THE BEMOAN

Jonathan M Chandler

The driver now out of the city cab the colour of a blue bird's egg pulled a large case from the boot and put it down beside one small one. He watched after Tru Beatty, at her effort in platform-heeled sandals and tight jeans to canter after a bus that was pulling out of the crossroads bus stop.

It was quite the bustle as the day drew to a close, folks stopping here to fill up on supplies before they took one of the four fingers of the compass and on to their evening destinations. Cars were lined up waiting to get gas into them, others were parked up all around the crossroads haphazard, the ground around all dirt and dust in the dirt and dust landscape. Small groups were walking in determined fashion to the general store of the petrol stop, or leaving the diner adjoined already loaded up.

Tru stopped in her tracks, adjusted the brim of her summer hat in one hand, let her handbag hang down from one handle with the other in a dejected manner, and her shoulders were down. A stamped foot would not have looked out of place. She watched the bus kick up a puff as it left for the rolling scapes to the south and onwards towards the sea. She came back to the cab driver and laughed. He might have been surprised at that, in light of missing her bus to Blua Haveno, but he knew the act.

He took off his glasses and dragged a forearm of his shirt across his eyes; a well built fellow with the air of a Clark Kent, but sweating just the same as everyone else, his slick hair more sweat than lacquer.

She waited for the glasses to go back on and then lifted at the brim of her summer hat and looked up at the sky and around the flats that surrounded the crossroads. Her voice had a light husk to it, "You're not going to leave a lady out here, I'm sure." The handsome woman let the late sun onto perfect tan skin, let it glow into her green eyes. She flapped the neckline of her blouse to air herself and then batted at imaginary dust on the thighs. And then looked back at the driver.

"They don't like city cabs coming this far out. I cross any further and that's my licence. How much is that worth?"

Tru came in closer and pulled a money clip out of her handbag. "How much do I owe you?"

"That's seventy five."

She raised an eyebrow and did a face, a face that was supposed to say either that was reasonable or that was a joke. She counted out eighty, suspecting it had been a lower number until the driver had seen the notes.

The driver took it and Tru kept the money clip in her hand, rotating it. The driver shook his head and went and got back in the car.

"Bullshit," she did mutter. She thought of her twin, Alice, and how she would be still in the cab, riding all the way down to the harbour town. This cabby had seen enough trouble to know what it looked like. Alice would have had the knack of letting him think maybe trouble could stick around in his life longer than the ride. A black magic Tru had never mastered.

She struggled her cases over to a timetable. Already some of the cars were leaving after having dropped off acquaintances for the bus. The numbers on the board didn't make a whole lot of sense to her and in whatever sense there was she couldn't see a single time later than now.

"Bullshit." She rustled in her bag and pulled out her mobile phone and checked the signal. Whatever interference made cellular phone contact impossible down in the bowl of Kratera City, out here they just didn't bother with any service. She considered the telephone wires on the poles, hugging the line of the road towards her destination.

Two groups passed her as was she went into the diner, their bellies loaded up with grub and coffee, and a second wave of cars would soon be away.

The heat of the day was starting to take its foot off the pedal, in here it had forgotten its manners to do so. By dawn the room would have barely cooled before the next sun would be piling in on top of it. Three ceiling fans were the only music in the place. Tru moved over to the nearest one, put down her cases, took a kerchief from her handbag, and mopped at her collarbone and forehead.

Some sat at tables by the windows, slatted blinds slicing animal stripes onto them. A man of fifty sat at the counter alone in work shirt and slacks of subdued blues and cheap loafers. In the mirror that lined the back wall behind the counter she saw the man looking, pause before forking some pasta into himself, and he held her gaze. She went over to a stool a couple away from his, making exaggerated 'it's hot' noises.

"You want the telephone," said the ancient man behind the counter as he ferried dirty plates to a window to the kitchens, his neck thin in a shirt done up to the top button. "Last bus, and the cab dumped you here." He poured her a glass of water that looked warm and was. "Might have been better off going back to town."

"Why, your phone not working?"

"We close sooner than your ride will get here."

Tru stretched out the toe of her sandal and studied it pressing against the bar at the foot of the counter. The man in blue looked at her briefly all the way bottom to top and forked some more food into his mouth. She waited. He looked at his watch and pushed his plate of pasta forward. "Box me that."

The old man took it and went through a door to the kitchen backwards and giving Tru a look as he went. She did her best to read it.

The man had slapped down a no, so she looked around at the other customers; a couple of groups numbering enough to fill cars entirely.

Tru took the money clip from her pocket and tapped it on the table as if to straighten it but so that the man would see it in his periphery. Nothing.

"What is it?" she asked, "You been home late to your missus the whole week already? Now you can't run an abandoned dame down to Blua Haveno, because there's no money in the world to make up for having to stick a lie on her. She see right through you?"

He turned slowly upon his stool to face her. His eyes came last, switching them from her visage in the mirror to the real item. "Maybe I just don't like you."

The dimple in his chin was not cute in a face that was long and slightly bulbous, the hair cut very short at the sides made his head look taller than it needed to. The man was not pretty enough to bat away a good looking woman without hating on women. Maybe it was Arab looking women he wasn't into. Tru put her money clip away and forgot about him as soon as she span on the stool to get another look at the room.

The door to the toilets came open. A short haired woman with eyebrows crafted to severe effect came out two steps and stopped. Over a white t-shirt she wore a loose summer suit with rolled up sleeves showing off tattoos on dark skin. She looked Tru over and then came in her direction. Maybe this was a pick-up spot.

The face on this woman was hard, just like the guy in blue. Tru turned on her stool and took up the glass of repulsive water. The woman came over and sat on the stool between her and the man but it was him the woman turned to.

Tru watched this unexpected pair in the mirror. If they thought the hum of the fans hid their voices it didn't.

The man said, "What's with the two cops out there by the phone booth?"

"Jesus, you para, or what?"

"Maybe. Let's go anyway. This crowd is thinning

out fast."

"It's nothing to worry about. There's a party up at the David place tonight. They're just watching to see if any faces come through."

"Lambert David? He only just went down."

"Yeah, and what does his boy do? A big fuck you to the cops, have a party, invite anyone you can think of. How are the porkoids supposed to know who it is you're meeting with if you're meeting with everyone?"

"Where's your invite?"

"Real faces," she scoffed, "So stop your worrying. No one's scoping for the like of us."

"Yeah, but they're looking." He tried to get a look through the window to the kitchens. "Where's that old fart with my nosh? Ah forget it." The man got up abruptly, looked at Tru once more in the mirror and she looked at her water like it was the most interesting thing she ever saw and the odd couple walked out.

One of the groups in the booths got up and so did Tru and followed them out. They went over to their car joking merrily amongst themselves. The man in blue and the woman in the suit were already pulling away in a shabby saloon, south towards Blua Haveno. She wasn't sorry not to be riding with them but since she'd gone inside the diner a few more cars had dispersed their ways out from the crossroads.

There was the phone booth across the way. A cop

out of uniform, if that was what he was, stood there in short sleeves and tie, hair parted but a little too long in the fringe and hanging down towards an eye. Resting herself on the hood of an unmarked four-door nearby was a similarly dressed female cop, if that was what she was, with hazel eyes and hazel straight hair and smoking a hazel cigarillo.

As Tru sauntered over laden with her cases the man cop stepped up between her and the telephone.

"Sorry lady, this one's out of order."

"So why are you standing next to it?" She dumped the cases around her.

The cop took his badge from a pocket and flashed it at her. "Waiting for a call, sorry lady." Tru reached for it but he put it away again.

"You see any other phones around here, officer?"

"Ask inside if you're desperate."

"Look I missed the bus."

"Yeah I know."

She looked at the woman cop but she gave nothing, just smoked as before, watching after a couple more cars leaving the area. Tru plonked her handbag on top of her other luggage and crossed her arms.

"There was a strange couple in the diner. Seemed worried about two cops out here, they just set off south for Blua Haveno."

The woman cop seemed interested. "That's where

you are headed. Right? You want us to give you a ride and we can be on the look out for these weirdoes at the same time."

"You wouldn't?"

"We're in the middle of something."

"What would that be?"

The man cop spoke up, "Police business."

"Is that so? Well if I get stuck here and you're staying here we may as well get to know each other."

"Let her use the phone," said the woman cop.

He stepped aside and presented a hand towards the phone. "Please be quick, madam. Wouldn't want to miss that call because you missed your bus."

"Fine, tell me what's riding on it and I might even have as much sympathy as you do."

"Police business."

Tru took up her handbag and looked in it. "You have any change?" She fished in her pocket for her money clip.

He looked at her impassively. Tru looked at the senior cop who turned her head away as if they'd never spoken and smoked.

"Alright. That's fine. How are you two supposed to make a call?"

"CB," he said, and he thumbed at their car bronze in the dusk coming on. "And like I said we're waiting for a call, not to make one."

"Can I use that CB?"

"To make a phone call?" He smiled and shook his head as lazily as the woman cop had looked away. "That's not how that works."

"Great. Well at least I can trust you to look after my luggage, if that wouldn't be too much a bother for you?"

He put his hands in his pockets, shrugged.

She walked back towards the diner and saw that it was now closed. She detoured towards the general store and went inside. No one was in there, shopping or paying for petrol or working the till. She went to the door and out again and looked at the cars that remained. Just a quarter hour ago there had been a score of vehicles parked up and now there were just three left: the cops' Kaprico, a bug-like Skarabo, and a classic sporty Barakudo.

The old man from the diner was there with a clipboard, looking at boxes tied to the top of the Barakudo, marking things off with a stubby pencil.

Tru came to him. "You run the store as well?"

"Yes," he said without looking up.

"You cook as well?"

The old man laughed and raised his hand. She looked past him and saw the flash of a palm from the driver's seat of the Skarabo as it pulled out and took off with a hearty thrum.

"Oh that's the cook going."

"He leave you to clean up?"

"Kind of."

"There's no one behind the counter in the store, I need some change for the phone booth."

"Oh right," the old man looked up. "You're the one who missed a last bus."

"Yes, you going south when you're done?"

"Oh no, I live up there above."

"I see, well can I get some change for the phone so I can call my sister?"

"Oh, I wouldn't want to be waiting here that long. Not here after dark."

"There's two cops over there, I'll wait."

"That's not cops. She's coming up from the harbour?"

"Yes."

"She'll be a while."

"She doesn't drive."

"Right, so how is she going to come?"

"She'll sort something out, she's that kind of a person."

"Good person."

"Debatable, but she gets things sorted."

"Yep." He went back to his clipboard as if the exchange was done.

"So can I get some change?"

"You really want to be here after dark?"

"I can always wait inside with you. Maybe even use your telephone."

"I use that one." He pointed his pencil at the phone booth across the road. Tru looked over there. The man cop was watching impassively.

"Alright, so I get some change and come and wait inside with you."

"Oh I don't know about that. Better if I drove you."

"You would?"

"If I had a car working. Mine's out back. Kaput."

"What's this?"

"His. Ishida's." The old man next pointed his pencil at a man pushing a two-wheeled handcart from a side door to the store with a couple more boxes on it, dressed in work shirt and trousers and with deck shoes incongruous to the look, and his spectacles had expensive designer frames cast in a semi-translucent yellow amber.

"His what, Anthony?"

"His vehicle. The lady is stuck here because she was late for the bus, and she wants you to drive her down to Blua Haveno, even though you aren't going that far."

Ishida took the towel from around his neck and daubed himself with it. He had an ageless look on him, maybe a young looking older man, or an older looking young man. The truth was that he had been born eight years earlier than Tru, and her now thirty eight.

He opened the door to the Barakudo and reached in and took out a pipe and then some matches from a shirt pocket and lit the pipe.

"Where are you headed? Mister . . . "

"Call me by Koji."

"Where are you headed to, Mister Koji?"

"Just Koji. Lighthouse. I'm helping over at the lighthouse for the rest of the summer."

"I didn't know they had lighthouse keepers anymore."

"They do if they pay for the experience."

"Oh?"

The old man Anthony handed the clipboard over to Koji Ishida. "There we go, that's all of it. Sign there please." He did and handed it back and the old man put the stubby pencil behind his ear so big in old age it near vanished. "Good, thanks son. Have a good summer. Say hello to Ortiz. Say hello to his wallet and tell him to bring it up here and pay what it owes and get the rest ready to lose on the cards."

"Thanks Tony."

The old man took the now empty trolley and shuffled it back towards the side door to the general store.

Koji looked at Tru, raised his eyebrows after the old

man and tilted his head at him for her benefit, in collusion about some element of the old man's character. She didn't like it but smiled anyway.

"Well how about that lift, Mr. Just Koji?"

"Well, there you're in luck." He went at securing the last two boxes with rope. "Just so happens I have to go down to the harbour and pick up said Ortiz who will now be four sheets to the wind."

"Who's he? The real lighthouse keeper?"

"Something like that." He finished with the ropes, "In we get."

She got in and he got in and she put her head back a moment and closed her eyes and huffed out some air to show her relief to him. The car started up with a deep gurgling throb that said it had speed but when they pulled out it was a reassuring and quiet turnover from under the hood, reversing and gliding out smooth onto the old tarmac. The sun was going now.

"Hell of a spot to get stranded in," said Koji. "I hear unkind things about who passes through this area at night. I've heard the old man advise people to hide out the back with the bins until they get picked up."

"So I'm not the first person to get stranded here."

"Always feels like you are the first and only to ever wind up that way, doesn't it? Yeah they say this is on the drug route as well. They make the old man come out sometimes and pump gas but they leave him alone well enough otherwise."

"Oh wait. My luggage. I left it with those two cops back there."

Koji slowed the car and turned it and they went back. When he saw the cases, the one smaller and the one larger, he said, "We'll have to try and fit it in behind the seats here. Boot's full, what little space it did have."

The back seat was paltry and had no leg space but enough for the cases. He stayed at the wheel and let her get out for the luggage and pushed her seat forward after her to make a route for it.

The man cop was stood rested against the booth with his arms crossed. The woman cop was inside their car. He stood and walked to Tru as she picked up her belongings but didn't help.

"Looks like you found some loose change."

"Thanks for all the help. Don't get cold out here waiting for whatever it is you're waiting for."

"I was looking forward to going through your stuff you nearly let off without." He watched her rump in her jeans as she loaded the cases. The cop leant down and spoke to Koji turned awkwardly in his seat trying to help her. "Nice ride I bet."

Tru straightened up as Koji pushed her seat back and she turned to the cop. "At least I finally found a man in this dive."

He sniggered. "Weak."

She got in and Koji pulled away for the second time and turned for the second time and headed them south for the harbour town.

"What was that?" he asked.

"Are they cops?"

Koji went to check in his rearview but couldn't because the cases blocked the view and glanced instead at the side mirror.

"I didn't really notice. Why do you think they were or weren't cops?"

"Well he had a badge."

"So that would make him a cop."

"Something deeply unpleasant about seeing a city cop not in the city."

"You a city person? Me too as a rule."

"I always say I prefer it but I spend most of the time down here at our cousin's place. With my sister. I can always leave whenever I want to. I'd say that's probably what stops me. You can't so easily now I bet."

"Leave the lighthouse?"

"I couldn't bear it. Signing up to something like that ahead of time. Is it your first time?"

"Yes, it suits me well enough so far."

"Mhm, and what are you normally?"

"Usually I'm an engineer."

She looked at him in the light of the dusk and the light of the panel instruments. "You ever come into town?"

"Blua Haveno? I do. You'll have to introduce me to your sister some time."

"Check out all the options before you commit, eh?"

"What?" He looked over with a half smile, embarrassed. "No."

She looked back to the road. "We're twins."

He looked her over, as if he was studying for how the sister would look, and his eyebrows were up and she saw it in her periphery and laughed.

"It always gets men excited, could you ever tell me why that is, Mister Koji?"

"Not really. How do you think when you think about other twins?"

"Well, I'm not a man, and if I was it would still be repulsive to me."

"I'm glad you missed your bus."

"You are?"

"You are an interesting person, Miss . . . "

"Miss Tru. Tru Beatty. Don't you ever think it's weird they always introduce themselves in films with a whole name?"

"You think so? I don't really watch a lot of films. Maybe it's just old films?"

"Don't you have a favourite movie?"

"Not really." He looked out at the patchy landscape of scrub interrupted with the odd tree or cacti, as if something out there would be a clue to an answer. Nothing was coming.

"Come on, there must be something?"

"Now I'm on the spot. I don't think one would exist before you asked the question."

"Maybe I should ask what's your favourite engineering feat?"

He laughed and then looked in his wing mirror, impelled at the memory of those two cops they had left behind loitering at the crossroads.

"What would cops be doing hanging about anyway, Miss Tru? Out for those marauders the old man's always on about?"

"I don't know, just something's on at the David place tonight."

"David Ortiz? What?"

"The lighthouse man? Your boss? Don't be silly. David as a last name. Lambert David."

"Who's Lambert David? Something big?"

"Wow, you don't watch movies, and you don't read newspapers."

"Just the engineering section."

"The engineering section?"

"There isn't one." He glanced at her, a tell that he was insecure about his feeble comebacks. "So what is he? Lambert David?"

"Just some kind of money criminal."

"Isn't that all of them?"

"No, there's the psycho criminals as well."

"Yes, of course. I'm being stupid again. It's been a long day."

"It's a good question. I wonder the proportion?"

"Of money to psycho criminals?"

"Yes. And then there's the passion criminals." She played at a space on her neck as if looking for a necklace there.

"Would you like the radio on?"

"I'm not so bothered. Hey you know that bus has got some headway on us. If this thing is as fast as it looks it should be, can you get me caught up with it? Alice is going to be sorely pissed at me when I don't step off at that bus stop, even more pissed when she drives out alone to that dive back there to find I'm not skulking around by the bins. And I do so hate the idea of her having to be there alone. Your stories of the place have put the willies up me."

"I thought you said she didn't drive."

"I do like a man who pays attention."

"Anyway, there's those two cops there tonight."

"Christ, I wouldn't want to subject her to that."

"Alright, we'll try and catch up a bit." He toed harder and the engine hungrily accepted and trilled and pushed them on.

The flats broke into low hills, the Barakudo dipping and rising and after some good time, at the top of a high point in the road, they saw ghostly faint the glow from the small harbour town had come into the sky now otherwise dark, and closer to them, a few rises distant, the tail lights of the bus heading that way before them, tiny but sure.

Tru, gone quiet in some small fear and thrill at their speeding, saw the payoff and perked, "We've got them. Koji, you showoff, we're going to make it in first."

"I never pushed it this hard on a road I don't know well. I hope you appreciate it.

"I thank you for not letting your male pride go to ruin."

They came down the hump and into a valley across the road where a cold-well stretched across before them, an isolated stretch of white fog.

Tru saw the faint tail lights of another car in front of them, inside the fog. Either unmoving or so outpaced by the speed of the Barakudo that it seemed so. If Koji saw them he made no sudden reaction to the breaks.

They went into the fog, the front of the Barakudo going into the other vehicle, the Barakudo glancing off, on two wheels then four, then off the road to the side and flipping and rolling twice and skidding out some twenty metres more into the undergrowth, sparse of plant and mostly dirt but rocky also.

The car was righted but ruined, the engine humming complaintively. Koji raised his hand in front of his face, turned it in the light from the control panel as if it were some object alien to him, then watched it float down to the ignition and flick off the engine. Each move he made came in a laboured half-time, and with that same delicate motion he looked to Tru.

Her door was already open and she gone. Either he had for some uncounted moments been passed out or she had been flung away in violence.

He tried his own door but that would not open. He looked again at both his hands, as if their state would tell of any injury. The hands were blurred. His glasses were off his face. He felt along his door and felt it where it crumpled. Then he undid his belt and put it aside and found it was twisted in the mounting and took the time to put that in order. In the same dazed slow-mo he managed the clamber to her side of the car and got out.

Lights from the other vehicle lit that fog from the inside and in the direction of his own car. A rugged swath of dirt made for a new path back to the road, littered with the broken boxes of the lighthouse's larder supplies, tins and cartons rent and torn and flattened and many still whole. He staggered that way, looking himself over and he saw blood on his work shirt on one side and down an arm. His small towel had stayed around his neck and he took that and dabbed at the blood and opened his shirt and felt inside and found none there and then he realised it was the arm that had been facing Tru in that passenger seat and that the blood was not his. It was on his knees and shins too where he had dragged himself over her seat.

He moved to the light, not in a stagger now but in a walk with tiny steps like an infant, dragging his feet through a rent bag of rice, spreading the grains into twin trails.

He called out, "Hoi!" Nothing.

Stepping onto the tarmac he got a better look at the saloon he had collided with. One side was hollowed in from the impact. He replayed the moment. The car must have been angled across the road, his Barakudo glancing off in a ricochet while this car had been spun where it sat. He looked back, at the foodstuffs tossed and ripped and scattered in his wake.

"You hurt?" The voice was a woman's with a hard edge. Startled he turned to the road again but too fast and staggered and sat on his backside. She came to him. A short haired woman in a summer suit. She offered a hand and he took it and he got up.

"You hurt?" she repeated.

"I don't know. I don't think I'm hurt. That's not my blood I don't think. My passenger."

"You got lucky. What about him?"

"She. It was a she. Are you hurt?" He looked her over standing unscathed in the headlights of her car.

"No, I was out of the car when you hit us. Out of the way when you turned us. Some speed up you had there."

"What were you doing parked in the fog?"

"Wild dog ran out. Your friend done for?"

"I just met her."

"Yeah? Your stranger then. She done for?"

"You said us?"

"Let's see about your new friend first. She dead?

"I don't know." He looked back through the passage of carnage that led off the road and then saw the woman in her summer suit walking that way and he followed her and asked, "You didn't see her? She got out already."

The woman said nothing, went to his car and

looked in the open door where Tru had been sat and then they both looked around into the dark.

"You hear that?" said Koji.

"Maybe, shhh." They listened and heard a groaning somewhere, not far nor too close. "You got a flashlight?"

"I do." He leaned into the car and popped the glove compartment open and took out a torch and turned it on and then led them out into the dark, swooping it over the wiry grasses and rocks.

The woman tugged on his sleeve. "No, more this way." They adjusted and moved again. "Hey, lady," the woman called. The groaning stopped. "You hear us?" They stopped walking. "You have to speak up. We only found you because of that whining."

"I think this way," said Koji. He walked on and they came to a few boulders piled up taller than a person and in a configuration like there had been some purpose in it.

They circled and saw Tru sitting on one of them, her handbag hanging from a shoulder was open, tissues spilling from it in a plume and strewn all about her in scarlet, her face a pure mess of blood, first from a nose that had gushed, and then from the trickle still coming that was wiped all around with her frantic cleaning in the dark. It was all down her face and neck and her blouse wet with it clung onto her breasts. She squinted into the torchlight and held a hand up holding blood red tissues and Koji dropped the light away.

"You got my nose broken." She spoke in a voice claggy with swallowed blood. "You've ruined everything." They did not know to whom she spoke and each took an arm and got her up and they started walking back to the road and she continued on. "It's a disaster. How could this have happened? This time of all times? It's typical. I was born to this. Always the same. I never get out of anything. You should see my twin. My Alice. Nothing ever turns out badly for her. Nothing. She carries on like she is depressed, like that was what she was born with. Her depression and my bad luck. It's a put on. She just uses it to get attention. And she always gets what she wants. She always gets whatever she asks for. And now she'll even have my face."

When they got back to the road Koji passed the torch to the woman and led Tru to the bonnet of the woman's car and sat her on it.

"Here, let me see." The woman put the light on Tru's face and Tru squeezed her eyes shut at the light and Koji held her head and inspected her. "It might not be broken. He put thumbs gently either side of her nose and felt and she winced. "We'll need a doctor to look at that."

"Yeah? Whatever gave you that idea? Forget it. Just

get me home."

"Still in a hurry are we?" Koji stepped back and the woman drew the light away.

Tru opened her eyes. "What's going to happen when Alice sees I didn't make it in off that bus?"

"Listen, Trudy."

"It's Tru."

"Tru. Listen, we're all going to be a little late out of this. Maybe we'll get lucky and those cops will come by."

The woman put the light on the side of her car that had been bashed in. The front wing had pierced the tyre and the wheel was askew on its axel and raised off the ground. "This road is dead this time of night. Maybe we can drive out."

"You're kidding?" said Koji. He had come to inspect the wheel, leaving Tru holding another wad of tissues on her face with her head back as people her age had been taught growing up.

The woman got in and tried the engine and it chugged and smoke came out from the bonnet and Tru got up from the hood and backed away. The woman turned off the engine and left it to hiss and ping. The glass in her window was gone. "Come on, push at least, let's get this off the road before we break someone else's nose off."

Koji went to the back of the car. The woman called

out, "Lady, go and help him."

"My nose is broken."

"It's fine," called Koji, "Just let the hand break off."

She did and he pushed and the car rocked but stayed on its three good tyres for the most part and the car was rolled off the tarmac and she steered it left of the virgin track in the wake of the Barakudo and down a slight incline.

"That'll do it," called Koji, but the woman ignored him and let it go on a good distance more before it scraped onto some rocks and stopped and she turned off the lights.

It was now dark in the cool fog patch and Koji went to Tru and did not at first see her and then saw that she was sat down at the roadside with the wad of tissues still on her face.

"Has it stopped?" he asked her.

She said something muffled back.

"Say again?"

She took the tissues away. "Can you hear it?"

"Huh?" Koji listened and heard faintly the sucking sound of a distant car travelling somewhere along the road. "Which way?" He turned left and right and couldn't discern that. He held out a hand and Tru held it and got up. "Right, you get out one side of this fog patch and I'll get out the other and we'll flag them down."

In a quick jog he went back the way they had come in. As the fog thinned he saw the lights coming on them fast from the top of that last rise. He kept to the side of the road and ran faster and waved his arms and called "Ho!" He cleared the cold-well as the car came upon him and then it was gone into the fog but had not faltered in its speed. He turned after it and stood there watching after the tail lights as they were engulfed by the fog and from in the fog he heard a thudding.

The lights came to a halt. As he ran back into the fog patch they moved off again and the car was getting only faster as it went onwards and out the other side and on towards Blua Haveno.

"Tru?" He ran towards where he thought the car had hit her and almost stumbled over a person there lifeless. Tru came to him out of the fog in the other direction. "They didn't stop."

"You get a look at them?"

"No."

"Plates?"

The torch beam came up from the side of the road.

"Christ!" said Koji, "I thought it was you they hit. There's someone else here. Is that the wild dog you stopped for? Did you hit someone?"

"No. You did."

"What?"

She put the torch on the man's body. The body was rag-dolled with an arm twisted awkwardly behind his back. Blood smears pulled away from him in various directions. There was a lot of blood, for being hit twice by a car.

The man's face, even with half of it pushed onto the floor and disfiguring him, she recognised, that hair and the dimple in the chin. "Oh it's you two." She looked at the woman.

"What you two?" said the woman.

"Back at the crossroads, I was sat at the counter, beside you."

"Oh yeah?" said the woman unimpressed.

Koji's hands floated around the man unsure what to do with them. "Why didn't you say anything?"

"Would that have brought him back?"

"You just left him in the road to get hit by another car."

"You having a go at me? Looks like it was you going too fast to start this off."

"That other car hit him too."

"Yeah, sure, after he was unable to get out of the way."

Koji got to his feet, almost stumbled dizzy. "I ... I can't believe this has happened." He stood stunned while his mind went over the implications, all the futures rushing in and competing for the one most likely where he was certain he was in prison for it.

To Tru the woman said, "Did they get a look at you?"

"At me? I don't think so. They took off fast."
"That's right. And as far as they know they just hit at best a dog and worst a person."

Koji seemed out of his trance at the words. "What are you saying?"

"I'm saying what you want to hear. That you didn't kill him. I'll go along with it."

"That's your friend I killed."

"No, it was the dog that got him killed for stopping us."

Tru put her wad of tissues in the torchlight and looked at it. "I think my nose stopped bleeding." Her voice was still muddy like with a bad cold.

"Alright," said Koji, "Let's think about this."

The woman was walking back to her car. "I'll get something to put him in, get him out of the road."

Koji came closer to Tru and spoke lower. "What do you think about this?"

"I think I want to get home and cleaned up."

"What does she care about you and me not taking the rap for this?"

"I don't know, Koji, maybe she doesn't want any cops involved. Maybe she doesn't care enough about this person on the floor to have to spend time over court and red tape. If she wants to say it was a dog I'll go along with it."

They heard the boot of the woman's car pop, and through a fog veil saw the patch of light where the torch beam was bobbing about and her taking some things from the boot. Koji held both his hands to the sides of his head. "I can't get my mind working."

"We can work it out, engineer it."

"Alright, well for now it doesn't matter. We'll just go along with it this way for now. Maybe in the morning we can make some sense on it."

"You think so? I'd say a lot of what comes down the line over this is going to depend a lot on what we decide right now."

They heard the boot of the car closing, watched as the torch started its path back their way. They waited without talking and the woman reconstituted in front of them with a large piece of canvas that had been folded into a square and a coiled rope over a shoulder. She held a shovel. She gave that to Koji. He held the shovel in awe like it was an Excalibur.

"We're going to bury him?"

"Those dogs out here, you never encountered the kind, I'll bet. If we don't get him covered they'll spend their whole night chewing him out of this." She gestured with the canvas.

"I thought just leave him in your car. The story is

that other car hit him. No, because of the injuries, two cars. Two other cars. And we came in and hit a dog."

The woman tilted her head and screwed her face at his suggestion. "I don't want that mess in my car."
"But it's totalled, and it was already a piece of junk."

"I don't want him in there. You want him in yours?"

"My car's a write off. I suppose we could."

"Look, I don't think we should be here the whole night. I think we should walk out. And I don't want anyone snooping around and gloating over my friend looking like that in the morning, taking pictures for the internet and selling it to the papers before the cops come in. That's beside the point. You're missing something here, mister. As far as anyone has to know he wasn't here. That's the cleanest way out of this."

"I saw you," said Tru. "I saw the two of you."

"It was busy back at the crossroads. Plenty people around. And who is going to track any of those people down to ask about someone who they aren't even looking for?"

Koji hefted the shovel. "She's right, Tru. We don't have to let this wreck our lives. It's done already. No number of cops investigating, inquiries, whatever, nothing is going to bring him back. A dog made this happen."

The woman started to unfold the canvas. "Yep.

Now he's getting it. Come on then, let's get it done. If we're lucky we'll be done before anyone else comes through, maybe even catch a ride when they do." She handed the torch to Koji and turned on another she had brought, long and hefty and more powerful. "Go out and find somewhere covered to start digging. By a tree or some rocks or something, somewhere where the disturbed ground won't be seen too well. And don't walk where you normally would, walk where your feet won't make a clear mark. With him wrapped up our feet will be heavy and we'll make a lot of tracks. Luck is our way because it's baked dry right now. If no one was looking for them they wouldn't see much, and with our story maybe they'll just imagine they're looking at a run for the dogs. No big forensics outfit will be dropping in, it's just a crash made by a dog. They see this mess in the road? That's dog meat. The others probably dragged it off and ate it."

Koji set off with his torch, paused.

"How deep?" "Don't go crazy but you'll need to put your back into it, city boy. Like I said, the ground's baked right now. Too shallow and the dogs will dig him out."

"Right. The dogs."

They buried Timmy Bridges and sat on some rocks and took a breather. Koji Ishida smoked his pipe and regarded the firmament above, moonless and clear.

"It's funny," he said, "How the heavens change, not depending on the weather or time of year, though of course that's true. As an amateur who doesn't know much of the constellations, it all becomes like this great mirror just for yourself."

Tru Beatty had his torch wedged between her knees lighting up her face. Using a pocket mirror she was using some of her beer to wet and dab at the blood with a tissue. "I'm going to stink like beer. God I don't even like beer."

Esther Moses had her feet up on the rock, knees bent and with elbows on her knees and her head down. Two empty beer cans sat next to her.

Koji took another of the last two beers from the carton. All six had survived in the boot of his car. He opened it and drank and looked up at the sky again.

"When everything is just fine you look up at the sky in awe of the Universe, at the beautiful mechanics of it, all that kind of thing. And when you are in a crap situation you look up and you think, in all of time and space, of all the things happening everywhere in all of the civilisations, I'm stuck right here in the jaws of some Earthly situation, like mostly financial or romantic ones. Like being caught in something so ridiculous. I'm not putting it very well. Do you know what I mean though?"

A car was coming along the road. It was only the second since the hit-and-run. Esther Moses raised her head. "You want that torch to be like a beacon?"

Tru switched it off. "I hadn't thought about that."

They all listened for the car and watched its headlights muffle when the car got to the fog and then it went away and onwards the same way as those others.

"What's your name anyway?" asked Tru. "I'm Tru Beatty. This is Koji Ichida."

"Mo," said the woman.

"Just Mo?" said Koji.

"You want my whole name for? I don't expect to be regular drinking buddies when this is done. You want to look me up in the phonebook?"

"Which phonebook is that? You called me a city boy

before. I wouldn't have taken you much for a country girl."

She slid off the rock and stood. She picked up the pickaxe. "I'm getting you out of a situation here. Your heads a bit together and now you're getting pushy, your nervous energy went out in the digging and you've got your beer and your tobacco. You'd still be out sitting in the road with a thumb up your butt if I wasn't here to take it out for you."

"Yeah, I suppose that's right."

Mo took the pickaxe and wedged it out of sight between the rocks. "I don't want to be a bitch about it. This wasn't what I was expecting to be doing tonight."

Tru was putting her mirror back in her bag. "To be fair, if it wasn't for you pulled up in a fog patch we wouldn't even have a thumb needs taking out."

Mo went next for the shovel propped beside Tru. She stood close to her. "I'm letting you off for how fast you seemed to be blazing down that road. As far as I care we're done with all the blaming. Like the man said, a dog did this, to all of us. Just a animal."

Tru sat quietly at that and Mo took the shovel and hid that as well.

Koji stood, put down his beer can and stretched and put a hand at the small of his back. He let out a noise and said, "Backbreaking work true enough. Tell me, Mo, sounds like you don't plan to come back for that car."

"That's right. I'm not. Car was his."

"Funny," said Tru, "Weren't you saying you didn't want him in your car?"

"Yeah it's my car. I'm saying it isn't."

Koji picked up his beer and drank again. "So how do we explain that? If we have two cars and only one with a driver. A missing driver they'll start looking around for and they'll find a missing driver alright."

"What happened is that the first car hit a dog. The second car also hit a dog and the first car as well. Where's the dog now? It must have crawled off and died somewhere. Who wants to be poking around looking for a dog? So what happened to the driver of the first car? When you were both unconscious in your car he must have taken his own off the road. Then panicked and maybe thought you were dead. When you got out you saw him further up the road hitching and getting in with someone stopped for him. You barely see him, just a man's figure maybe. Your head was ringing, eyes all fuzzy, can't see for the fog. Then he's gone and you're here by yourself."

"Who's going to pick up a hitcher out here in the night?"

"I don't know, ask the driver. You want to stop hypothesising for a minute and just ask what it is we do next?"

"To be honest," said Tru, "I'd rather I wasn't here either. I mean I don't need it to be known I was here. I don't have to be, your car doesn't need a passenger."

"That's fine," said Koji. "Except Anthony Elias saw me taking you. And those two cops as well. And half the blood out of your head is all over the seats."

"Ah shit." Tru flapped her arms like an annoyed child. "As soon as we decided to bury Mo's friend we screwed up. It's too complicated now."

Koji drank long on his beer. "Too late for that. It is what it is. I think we need to ask Mo what it is we do next."

"We take a piss," said Mo and she moved off around the rocks and rustled a short distance through the brush. Koji moved in close to Tru and spoke quietly. "Great, now she has our names and what do we know about her?"

Tru spoke back not as quietly. "Whatever. I'm too tired now. What are you worried about? If she's the big bad wolf, us little piggies are caught right out in the open."

"Yes, kind of feels that way. Well, what do you think? Story's good enough? This way I don't have to go to court over anything."

"Whatever you want."

"I'm exhausted too, but she isn't. You think this wasn't in some way how this was supposed to have turned out?"

"What are you talking about?"

"I think the dog we just buried was getting buried either way."

"What?"

"Her window was gone out from the inside. You think he bled before he even got out? I don't know. I guess I'm tired just as you are." He went at his beer.

Tru watched the rhythmic pumping in his throat as he drained the last. "I think I get you," she said. "Quite a set of tools to have in the boot of your car, wasn't it."

"Yes it was," said Mo suddenly close again and Koji dropped the empty can at the surprise. Mo puffed in derision. "I can't believe you two didn't already ask, which made me think you were thinking exactly what you just said you were thinking."

"It's probably nothing," said Tru. "We're just tired. And anyway," she directed the question at Koji, "What business is it of ours anyway, right?"

"No no," said Mo. "It's good you asked. Truth is we were out here to dig something up. The only person who knew where it was, was the dog now in that shallow grave. You think people like us are all just cold blooded killers or something. Trust me, you already seen how annoying it is to get rid of someone. So it would have to be a pretty good reason, and you sure as hell don't parade around with them in public before you'd do it."

"Oh God, I'm so sorry Mo," said Koji and a laugh came on him awkward. "It's this whole stupid situation, the accident."

"Yeah I know. This thing has cost me more than you know, but in my business you cut your losses and move on. Listen, it's all going to work out. The thing we need to do now is get out of here before dawn. We get out and the rest takes care of itself. You stick to the story like I said and nothing's to worry about."

Tru stood. "That part I like. The getting home."

"Right," said Koji. "So what do we do? Hitch? We've only seen three cars this whole time. Might not be another soul comes this way until the morning. We can't get down to Blua Haveno before dawn."

"You're right," said Mo. "So we walk it. We'll walk out the other way from the road and keep going until we get near the coast. There's always something along a coast. What do think, honey, you can handle it in those shoes?"

Tru instinctively bent her knee up and reached and played a finger around the foot in her sandal and held Koji's arm for balance with her free hand.

"Don't see that there's much choice in it."

A small tablecloth taken from the boot of Koji's car was tied up into a papoose that he loaded with a few supplies from the goods scattered in the wake of the accident, and Mo went to her car and got a duffel bag and looked to do some scavenging the same but there wasn't much that had survived that was any good without being cooked first. All the drink they had was the few beers Koji had bought to have with David Ortiz the actual lighthouse keeper. The main salvage was some biscuits, big dry things, like something that would have ended up weavel-ridden that sailors would have scoffed back in the days when they'd be at sea on the longer jaunts.

Tru took out her luggage and insisted on bringing it, so as to leave no trace of her being there, and they set off walking through the brush with Koji up front and Tru in the middle and Mo with her torch coming up the rear, like a solemn procession in thoughts of hopes and wishes that the nights events would have as little consequence on their lives as they wished for, with varying degrees in the belief of such an outcome.

After some ten minutes they had stopped and turned off their torches and looked back to the road and seen one last car on its way down to Blua Haveno, already jealous of that life carried inside, in comfort in its vehicle, and they watched as it did not stop when it went through that fog patch that had already diminished since their event, but which was not yet ready to give up any secrets to this new traveller, and the car went on. And they turned and turned on their torches and went on.

They did not get much further more before Tru tired of carrying the cases as the others knew she would. She stopped by a patch of cacti densely packed and swung the larger of the two like a discus and landed it amongst those thorned plants irretrievable. She took instant regret that she had not first changed at least that blood-ruined blouse.

Tired and quiet they walked on, the three strangers a tripartite moving through the landscape, as much a part of the cosmic machinery above them, to which Koji had contemplated, as that starry heaven itself; some tiny part of the cog-works in support of that grander scheme, not extraneous to necessity, but equal in import, each lost desert wanderer, each leader of nations. The thoughts of these three were consumed by appreciations of having fallen suddenly outside of the established paths, paths of lives that had been forged by themselves and by society but by which that greater cosmos was indifferent and encompassing both.

Within the hour the ground underfoot was starting havoc on Koji's feet in those boating shoes, but not enough yet to have him falter greatly in his timekeeping. He had though started to wonder about that dead man's shoe size. Behind him Tru was starting to succumb to her own struggle with her remaining luggage, and a gap was starting in between them.

"Should we take a break yet?" said Tru. The voice cutting almost violently into an air that had been so silent as they had wandered as somnambulists. Koji stopped and turned and waited for them to cover the small distance between them. He flashed his torch on his watch but that was broken. "How long has it been?"

He saw Mo put torch to her own wrist. "Only an hour and half. Just over. Let's push on if we can, there's still a while to go. You want to give the lady a hand with that luggage?"

His muscles still ached from digging into that hard earth, but there was nothing to do but to do as Mo suggested and he took the case from Tru.

"What have you got in here? The Elgin Marbles?"

"Oh forget it." Tru took back the case and he didn't protest. She opened it quickly and took something and put it in a front pocket of her jeans and took a shawl and then closed it. With no cacti to nest it in she merely tossed this one a few feet into the brush.

"I've been headed this one way," said Koji, "But that's just been a direction I imagined in my mind." He looked up again at that star map. "Should have been checking the navigation systems. I like the idea of that, though I wouldn't really know what I was looking at." He scanned around trying to pinpoint the Pole Star. The sky dizzied him. He had spent five fruitless minutes back at the car looking for his vanished glasses and gave up under the pressure of his companions ready and waiting. It might be his best look at the Milky Way and all the rest of it he had ever had, and here he was half blind.

"I think we're alright," said Mo. All three stopped and looked around at this landscape unknown to them, seeming to them not trodden for generations, not even by some shepherd or other, or perhaps never, not even by early hominid, and all did doubt Mo's words. And yet within five minutes more Koji stubbed the flimsy toe of one of those sailing shoes on old and disused track-line and they gathered and looked at it.

"That's the old track line," said Tru.

"Yes," said Koji, "It seems so. I don't know the area well enough to know about that. How old?"

"I don't know, fifties or sixties or seventies maybe they got rid. Must have saved someone somewhere some money."

Mo traced it along with her torch. "And that goes all the way to Blua Haveno?"

"Used to."

"We could follow it in," said Koji.

Mo put her torch to Koji and he flinched at that and she put the beam down to his chest. "That wasn't the plan. You want to turn up there at dawn looking like a band of fugitives? Maybe this goes straight to the office of Wilford Lebeau."

"Yeah, who's that?"

"Local cop," said Tru. "Plain clothes, bent."

Mo had started to walk along the track. "You know another kind?"

The pair stayed watching her.

"Where are you going?" said Koji, "If you don't want to be going that way?"

"Water tower up ahead, maybe we can see a way if we get up there."

The three of them went there and Mo started up the ladder and Tru offered to hold her bag but she declined and went on up, and Koji decided to go up after her. Tru huddled down beneath the base of the tower in as comfortable spot as she could find in the long grasses there and propped her head on her handbag and curled up and pulled her shawl over her face and shoulders.

At the top of the ladder they circled the tower on the narrow walkway and stood looking out to the distance, which they imagined to be towards the sea and saw there a single light in the void.

"A ship?" said Koji.

"No. A house. It's the David place."

"Who is that? Tru said something about him."

"Yeah, what she say?"

"I don't really remember. It was when we were talking when I gave her the lift. Just chit chat. Wasn't really paying attention."

"And where do you know her from?"

"I was just giving her a lift. So who is David?"

"Lambert David, the place belongs to his boy now."

"Well, it's something to head for."

"I'd rather we look for somewhere else, but from what I heard their place is pretty isolated. It's up on the cliffs that way."

"Why you'd prefer somewhere else?"

"He's got a party on tonight. You want to turn up looking like this for a house full of people to gawk at? I'd rather not play the circus clown. You?"

"Not really, but I'd say they have a phone. And if there's people there's cars and maybe a ride out. Look, by the time we get out there maybe it's cooled down a bit."

All she did was let out a contemplative sigh in response and he paused a while thinking of the words to say.

"I don't really know what business you were on tonight and I promise you I don't care. Let's say the three of us start walking out there. If you choose against it you can carry on going down the coast. And Tru and I will make out like you were never in our company, just like we planned it out."

"Maybe. I'd have been happier if you hadn't said the word promise. There's no such thing as promise in the world. It's an idea people have, that the rules of the world have no interest in. I do like that you are trying to get rid of me now, that does have promise."

"That's not fair."

"Probably not. Not much fair about this night, is there, Koji san?"

He looked at the light at the David place. "Does it look far?"

"Things are always further than you think they are.

It always takes longer to get out of them than you planned for."

"Let's go and tell Tru."

He went down and Mo followed down and they found Tru amongst the grass, sandals pushed off, a snore coming from her blood clogged nose.

Koji spoke low, "How did she manage to sleep with all this that's gone on? You think you could cope with some sleep?"

"Maybe."

"Would give us some more time for those party goers to clear out of that David place."

"So that's decided the way we're going?"

"That's it for me I think, Mo. If you and Tru want to concoct something else then go for it."

"We'll see. Try and get some sleep."

Koji toyed the light from his torch around the dry grasses at the foot of the tower. "Aren't you worried about snakes? Scorpions or something?"

"That would be some bad luck. You look like a big dinner for a snake."

She found her spot and flicked off her torch and rustled into it while Koji loaded his pipe. When it was lit Mo was breathing slowly and then he went back to the ladder and went up. He took off the papoose and unloaded it and put the tablecloth around his shoulders and sat crosslegged on the gangway with his back against the old water tank that had served a world long gone.

He smoked and waited and thought about sleep, watching the lights at the David place and hoping there might be enough causality in its boring constancy for a feeling of slumber to come upon him, but he sat a long time awake listening to the metal ping of the cooling structure behind him, watched as car headlights every so often were taking their leave of the party and going away into the night, quite unknowingly watched from afar.

Dawn had cracked open a new day's account over beyond the David place and out to sea, the incoming heat dismissing the night cool of the water tower and Koji from his bird's nest, the sounding of his feet on the ladder stirring Tru into joining his wakefulness.

Mo was already sat up in the grass, her duffel bag still across her shoulder. Perhaps she'd slept that way. Tru clucked and swallowed at the filth that had her nose clogged and useless. She put on her sandals and stood and went to find a spot to piss on and took her remaining tissues from her bag and did her best to clear her nose out while she squatted. When she got back to the others they were eating those biscuits no one could believe Koji had spent money on. When hungry and with nothing else they did a good enough job but Koji was eating his so slowly it was clear he was forcing it, the reality of a new day making him sick of stomach, wondering at the foolishness of their actions back in the covering dark of the night.

Tru declined to even try them. They passed around that last can of beer they had kept until this morning and in that she did join them. They were all three dusted-up and dirtied well but Mo had somehow managed the whole escapade with unbloodied clothes. In the daylight Tru might have seen the hue of Mo's suit was different to that she'd seen her wearing at the crossroads diner, but she wasn't expecting that and did not notice that.

The front of Tru's shirt was darkened enough to look like it was a pattern put there by the manufacturer. She had it untucked, to disguise best she could the crotch of her jeans where in the car she had sat in her own blood after the accident.

She undid a button of the stiff blouse to show a pendant. She'd not worn it during the accident but she licked at it as if horrified this artefact might be besmirched in any way. It was something that looked like an actors mask of ancient Greece, with a laurel on its crown and with chub cheeks and little pig eyes. The mouth was agape like a love heart, a grin that was mocking, the joy in it only at the expense of another. She buffed the metal with a hem of her blouse, wanting it to match the shine she had for it in the eye of her mind.

Mo handed her the beer dregs now down below a

third. "Finish that. Koji here wants to go out to the coast, there's a big house out on the cliff there."

"It's the closest thing," said Koji. "This morning I can't say I saw a damned other thing anywhere as near. Or even much of a damned other thing at that."

Tru drank the beer out quickly to get that over with and threw the can into the grasses.

"I know where that is, everyone round here knows that. The David place. Fine by me." She went and took up her shawl and her handbag. "We should get a move on. Right about now I'd say someone may have noticed our cars already."

"Might not," said Mo. "That part of the road, nothing to slow for, they might see a flash of something and wonder. Might be days, longer. But let's say they did. Lot of nosy cops seem to be hovering around these parts because of that party they had at where we're now going to."

"Also worth to bear in mind that Tru and I might already had folks report on us not turning up when we should have."

"Not for me," said Tru. "I was making out last night that my sister Alice was expecting me, but that was just me trying to get someone to drive me. You know, you humanise the story a bit. She's not expecting me, but I have to be back there as soon as possible. And discretely."

"Oh yeah?" said Mo. "So what's this story?"

"It's complicated. You know, man stuff."

"Fair enough, not our business. And you, Koji? Who's waiting on you?"

He was quiet a moment, sullen at the news that he was speeding last night over a ruse. He mustered the energy, "Ortiz the lighthouse keeper. I was supposed to pick him up in the harbour. He'll have had a skinful. Anyway, the lighthouse was going around in the night so I know he got back there somehow.

"They don't automate that?" said Tru. "That's kind of old fashioned, isn't it?"

"If they upgraded it they couldn't get sucker city boys like me exercising their boyhood dreams for a summer or winter season."

"I hope they pay good," said Mo. "Some holiday."

"Yeah, I know it's daft. Even more daft is that they call it voluntary, but you have to pay for the opportunity, pay for Ortiz to have his boots full every night. Well, if he was drunk enough not to be worrying last night, he's an early riser, and maybe will be soon enough. Where's that boy with the pipe and my breakfast?"

"Come on then, let's get it done," said Mo and she crossed the long abandoned tracks and back into the sparse brush in that dry land.

Koji offered his hand as if to let Tru go first and they

fell in together and behind.

"Why didn't we ask her?" said Tru.

"Ask what?"

"Ask if there's anyone waiting on her, concerned at her not turning up. We just assumed not."

"She's certainly a kind of person who seems to have all her poker outs played in her mind, all the odds at hand."

"She even has better shoes for walking in."

The morning yawned wider and hotter. Mo had taken off that summer suit jacket, hung it across her duffel bag, and walked in her white t-shirt with rolled-up sleeves, showing off the tattoos and shapely arms. The others walked behind, watching that sweat patch on Mo's back spread. Tru without her summer hat lost in the night had her shawl tied up like a Bedouin head scarf and Koji used that little dirt and blood flecked towel of his to mop and busy at his brow and neck, the two disciples in shock under the glare of the day.

The David place loomed closer, a modernist build with plenty of glass. There was no gate at the foot of the long winding drive, nor fence for there to be a gate in. As they approached cross country they saw one car leaving from the aftermath of that party that had raged the whole night. It was a long classic vehicle for carting the monied people, with a driver in front and maybe two or three in back but their faces all in shade.

In instinct Koji took to crouching but the two women walked on brazenly, and if the occupants had seen them they made no falter in their journeying away from this place. And that left no vehicle at all up by the house.

The trees were less sparse up here along the cliffs, and beyond the other side of the road and not too distant to the right of the house, the largest topped a small rise and in the dell behind it two figures were crouched in camp.

The reporter was a man in the early part of his forties. The journalist with him was a woman another ten years on from that plus a bit more, though she did not look it, her straight shoulder length hair and dark glasses doing well to disguise where the creases were starting in. It was embarrassment at still being out on these grubby details that kept her careful of her appearance, kept her dyeing her hair. She felt the strain of the night gone kicking in, but the more the reporter complained at the same duty the younger she felt. She lay back in the roots of the tree, wrapped up in a long duster coat, head on her small army surplus shoulder bag, thinking of the office, and how, despite the squalor of the field job, if it ever came to being a full-time desk monkey would be the day she quit.

The reporter was constantly fiddling with his floppy hat, pushing his curls up inside it. He was already changed into a polo shirt and small shorts like he was eager to get out and get to a tennis appointment. He was wedged further up in the roots, looking over at the David place, flipping through his notes.

She opened an eye. "Any coffee left?"

"Just water. Well, I'd say we're done now anyway. That's his man Lawver Carrauza driving away with the last of the guests." He studied his lists. "Nah, there's still the piano man, and I never saw Schleifer come out. Always last out. Them two must still a piece."

"Well, relax for a bit, will you? We're not hitting press until tomorrow earliest. Another wasted night. Everyone smart was already out splatting the morning stands with it."

He slid down to come in sat beside her. "And with nothing new for us to add, that's no story at all." He dug in his rucksack and pulled out two paper cups and a bottle of water, then stuffed in his removed trousers and shirt and a small jacket from the ground. He poured them both water and he passed her one of the cups and she propped herself up to an elbow to take it.

"Salutoj," he toasted, and they drank. "That's the gamble. One day we'll stay and get that story they others didn't, right?"

"You should follow your instincts, Mitch. You copy my style because of my track record. That's been a few years now since it paid off. Editors have a very very short memory."

"That why you keep those awards all lined up on your desk?"

"Why else would I want that junk hanging about?"

A third figure approached them, crouched along the rise to keep her out of view from the house. The photographer was younger than them and was not white and struggling less already with the heat.

"Get anything good?" asked the reporter and he went in his bag to get another of those cups and started pouring water.

The photographer bopped down and went into her camera bag and the journalist sat up fully when she saw the haste in the movements. "What's going on?"

The photographer nodded at the direction of the road and the reporter ditched that third cup of water and his own and with the journalist they clambered back up to look out on the road.

He took off that floppy hat of his and clutched it in his both hands in front of himself. "What is it?"

"There," whispered the journalist, "Coming up the road."

The photographer was up beside them now and had her lenses ready and was soon snapping a record of these three dirtied and bloodied fugitives manifested out of the scrublands.

"Oh shit the bed," said the reporter, "Is this our night's story coming our way?"

At the porch Esther Moses went up the steps and approached the tall and wide door in the columned shade there. Slim windows ran along the top of the wall and were too high to see inside of.

Koji stayed out in the sun, hesitant to cross that border into the shadows that might bring some new reality. Tru sat down on one of the low walls either side of the steps, had her shoes off and a dirtied and scratched foot up on a knee, massaging at her heel.

By the door a handle hung on a chain. "Like flushing a turd," said Mo as she pulled on it and made a not unpleasantly toned bell ring inside the residence. She rang it a second time and then took off her duffel bag from her shoulder, revealing the stripe of sweat where it had lain, and then slipped into her suit jacket. No-one was coming. She looked to the others. "Great, looks like everyone just left."

"That can't be true," said Koji. He came up the steps

to join her. "If anyone in that car saw us coming to their house they'd have stopped and seen to what the hell was going on, to see three savages as us popping up out of nowhere on foot."

"Two savages," said Tru. "You hid on the floor."

"They never saw us," said Mo. She sat down on the top step.

Tru got up and went back out into the sun, looked up at the second floor balcony and shielded her eyes at the glare of half a morning sun staring over the roof, getting a useless view of the windows in that curved upper floor, windows of tinted glass looking jet black against the white of the walls.

Koji went up the steps and put his hand on the chain and yet did not pull on it, just held his hand there. The action might summon some person from inside, to break the seal on the lawless world that they lived in, that would cease to be upon the first meeting with any other person save a hermit who had no interactions with that outside world. And the occupant of this place with their raging night parties was not that hermit-like personage.

"What do we do?" he said. "Wait? I don't know I've the strength in me to walk out of here."

Tru came back into the shade, dragged herself with deflated shoulders and a sour puss on her, back to where she had sat before, undid her shawl and laid back on it with her legs dangling onto the steps and said, "I think we've done enough crimes to warrant one more."

"What?"

"We have to break in," said Mo. "Fine. Maybe there's more wheels in the garage."

"Hold on a minute," said Koji. "I think we're in deep enough already, don't you think?"

Tru raised herself up with exaggerated effort. "I think the idea is perfect. This way I never have to have been here at all."

"What's this disappearance obsession?" said Koji who stood with his hand still on that handle.

"None of our business," said Mo standing. "The lady doesn't want the hassle of talking to anybody, getting in the papers. Maybe she's a face."

"Papers?" Koji let go of the handle. "Why would we have to get in the papers for hitting a dog?"

Tru laughed heartily like she hadn't since the evening at the crossroads, some twilight world that may as well have been another altogether. "You're certainly the city boy, Koji. You think a place like Blua Haveno has anything better to write about? People get fed up of human smuggling stories, how does that really effect them? Refugees just get rounded up and shipped out anyway. And then the big papers up in Kratera, under the thumb of corruption, so much they can't talk about, just desperate to run anything weird from out in the provinces. Lot of column space to fill. And Koji, I'm not A-list, but Mo's right, I'm a face."

"Alright," said Koji, too tired even to ask about how. "Let's just have a little look around at least."

They went to the side of the house. There was a sturdy door set in a white wall that acted as a perimeter to the back of the place. The wall circled out to the cliff and further and overhung it and was impassable that way. Koji tried the door but it did not open. He leant his back against it and put a slight bend into his knees. He tapped a knee and said, "One," and then cupped his hands in demonstrating the next foot hold, "Two," and then tapped his shoulder. "Three. Up and over." He went back to cupping his two hands into a nest.

Mo readjusted the duffel bag on her shoulder and came and placed a boot on his knee and then put the other into his cupped hand and then the first foot onto his shoulder and Koji pushed upwards the foot in his hands and she clasped onto the top of the wall above the gate and hauled herself up as Koji pushed her higher and then the wall had her weight and she dropped down to the other side. They waited a moment and they heard a latch being undone and the door swung open. They walked through to the rear of the house.

At the back the outer wall turned to panes of glass to show off the ocean view. A real sun trap. There was a pool in the decking and loungers and tables strewn around and much detritus and glasses and empty bottles from a party scene from this night gone. The rear of the house was lined with dark glass both on this level and the one above, where on an overhanging balcony the only sign of people was more fallout left in their wake from the night's shenanigans.

They all three in their thirst went their own ways wandering around checking bottles and draining out what they could find and Tru found a platter of discarded party foods already wilting and watched a large black hornet with grey stripes pondering some seafood. She looked sharpish to the house. "You hear that?"

Koji looked to Mo who was already at the windows peering inside the dark glass through a cave made of her hands, and asked her, "You see anyone in there, Mo?"

"Piano," said Tru. "I can hear piano."

Koji listened through the waves crashing far below onto the rocks and fenced that noise and then he heard it too. Someone tinkling in a way you would hear in a posh restaurant. "Piano," he said. He put down an emptied bottle as his reaction to being caught the trespasser.

Tru took the water from him and drained what still remained in the glass in one swoop. She barely turned to see where to set it, dipped her knees, and put it down on the chest-bone of a woman in her mid-twenties who lay zonked out on a chaise-lounge beside them. The woman's hair was still done up immaculately with multitudinous hair pins and was wearing a party dress with a high collar and wide belt. She didn't stir.

"We got hit by a dog," said Tru.

"I'm sorry, you what?"

Mo stepped in towards them. "We got into an accident out on the highway last night. Totalled both our cars. A wild dog ran out between us."

"Oh Jesus, how bad was everyone hurt?" He was looking at all three of them up and down and the blood on Koji and Tru.

"Busted nose maybe?" said Tru. She tweaked at her nose. A stark bruise was making a line across the bridge and over her cheekbones. "I guess maybe not, but it bled like hell."

"Yeah, I can see you had no airbags. Christ." He looked again at the two others. "Anything else broke? I don't know if saying you got lucky is the right way to put it."

Koji regarded the bloodstains on himself, Tru's blood from where he had crawled across and out of his car, or was some of that from Bridges? "That's the dog blood," he said wooden.

"Everything's alright," said Mo. "Where's the phone? I want someone to come and get us."

"You do?" said Koji.

"Sure, I'll get you a ride into Blua Haveno, or your lighthouse, or wherever you want. My man shouldn't take too long to get here."

"He won't? You never told us about this. Where is he then? The harbour? Must be worried sick you didn't turn up last night."

"It's alright, wasn't expecting me back."

"No we'll get a taxi to come out, don't worry. You heading up to Kratera now I expect? Don't put yourselves out. Maybe we can get a ride with one of these two?"

"We're headed up to Kratera ourselves," said Trevor. "Glatz' man will take us when he's back." To Mo he said, "I'm sure you could get a ride with us."

"How long is he going to be?" said Mo, "This butler guy?"

"Yeah I see your point, a while. He's gone up to Kratera just now. We were planning to get some sleep here while we wait for him. Maybe it's us who can get the ride with you?" He raised his chin in a motion towards the girl already asleep.

"No, we'll take these two," said Mo. "I feel

responsible for seeing this through with them now I caused them so much misery already."

"It was you who hit the dog?"

"Yeah, in a fog patch of all the places for that to go down. These two came in behind and smashed into us."

"I'm just as responsible," offered Koji. "We were speeding. Stupid of me. Never assume an empty highway is an empty highway."

"No it was me," said Tru, "For hurrying you up like that."

"Don't worry," said Mo, "We aint suing you."

"So it was you two together?" asked Trevor. He was looking over Koji in those work clothes and deck shoes.

"Yeah, I was with him." Tru dipped and pushed the woman's feet aside and flopped herself down at the end of the chaise-lounge. She looked at the young woman. "You two an item?"

The woman stirred slightly and the empty glass slipped from her chest into the nook in her arm and she woke then and carefully took it and held it and studied it and then looked at Trevor and then Tru and then her eyes came open more and she shifted herself higher on that half-couch.

"You want to answer the lady, Sofia?" said Trevor.

"What? Jesus, what the hell happened to you?"

"They hit a dog."

"They what? What are you talking about?" She looked more carefully at the lady sat there. "You're one of those sisters." She looked at Trevor. "Your one?"

"No, this is the sister."

"How come you're all covered in blood? What happened?"

"They hit a dog."

Glatz came back into the room laden with a tray with several cups and a pot with coffee and with the new edition of the Krateran Times tucked under his arm. He came over to a low table. "Bachelet, clear some space here."

Trevor went over and helped.

"What kind of dog?" asked Sofia.

"Wild one," said Koji.

Sofia sat up and put her feet to the floor and regarded these two others. "What kind of dog is a wild dog? You know, the make. I mean, the breed of it?"

"Sofia," said Trevor. "You see these people have had a car accident and you are asking about what type dog it was?"

Glatz had poured himself a coffee and the others drifted over to the good smelling brew. Tru was eyeing the newspaper tucked under his arm, trying to get a look at the headline and Glatz saw her.

"Yes, I'm sure they'll be all over this party. Lambert

led away from court just two days ago, and here's me having a party. What do you think they'll make of that?"

"I couldn't say."

"Poppus cockus, of that there is no doubt." He started walking towards a spiral staircase. "Help yourselves. I'm getting dressed."

"I'll use your phone, alright?" said Mo.

"Certainly," he said as he got to the staircase. "Whatever you want." He paused with his foot on the lowest stair. He looked between Trevor and Sofia and took a good slug of his coffee. "Why didn't you two open the door when it rang? You made these poor souls into trespassers."

"I thought Lawva was still here," said Trevor.

Glatz flopped his hand at him and carried on upwards.

"I'm imagining a kind of mutt type thing," said Sofia. "What do you call them? You know, like those mongrelly street dogs, non specific kind of breed. I always think they look splendid, more than those small expensive things people pay for. And probably more healthy. Those bred things always have a lot of illness. Was it that kind of dog?"

"We didn't look too close," said Mo. "What with its guts out and the jaw off, it didn't look so splendid. Where's the phone?"

Trevor looked around. "I did see one."

Sofia pointed at the main double doors to the room, "I made a call in the night, it's out in the reception area."

Mo moved off that way and Koji started walking with her and she stopped and put a hand on his chest.

"Stay and take your coffee."

They were all quiet in the pause and then he nodded and went and took his coffee. The four that remained stood around the table and watched Mo go out of the doors and she looked back at them as she went out.

Trevor looked between Koji and Tru. "You two an item?"

Koji was still looking at the door, as if staring at it would tell him about the call being made.

Tru laughed but it was slightly forced and Koji took the cue and stopped looking at the door. "Me and Koji here? Or are you implying the man's smitten with our new friend out there?"

"She is wonderful," said Sofia.

"I meant you and Koji."

"Oh no, we just met. Koji was giving me a ride to Blua Haveno. I missed the bus at the crossroads."

"Ugh," said Sofia. "You'd not be the first. It happened to me once. I was only nineteen. Creepy place to get stuck by yourself at night."

"Oh, when was that?" asked Tru. "At least a year ago?"

"The nice old man there took me in though while I waited."

"More than he offered me. I guess he likes his woman company young." She looked at Trevor.

"How is Alice?" said Trevor.

"Is that all your own blood?" said Sofia. "How are you even standing?"

"Good question." Tru took a seat on a couch.

"That's not all her own blood," said Koji. He'd been sipping his coffee constantly and looking at the doors and made a high pitched sucking noise because his cup was empty and Sofia giggled and he poured some more coffee.

"That's dog blood?" asked Trevor.

"We had to move it," said Tru, "And these two were too chickenshit to help much."

Sofia put down her cup. "Well," she smoothed her skirt for effect, "I'm glad you're not her old man in that case." She sat down beside Tru.

"And how is it you met this bum, Sofia?"

Sofia smiled. If she thought there was malice in all the barbs coming at her she hid her understanding of that. "I used to go to all his concerts."

"Oh, a groupie?"

"No, I'm a critic, it was work. But yes, if I wasn't a

fan of this man's talent I wouldn't see how that would work."

Tru looked to Koji, "Would you sit? I know you've had a rough night, but you're unsettling me with that stiff look on you. The hard part's done." Koji nodded as if he wasn't really listening, was instead attentive to some internal record, and stayed stood there. Tru turned back to the girl, "So how do you get to be a music critic? Is that music school or writing school? Or nepotism? How does that work?"

Trevor fumbled at his trouser pocket. "You're reminding me of your sister." He pulled out a pack of cigarettes. "I'm going out for a smoke." He turned for the doors to the cliffside pool area. To Koji he asked, "You smoke?"

Koji nodded and walked after him. He paused to look back at the doors that Mo had left through, "Long phone call."

"I'd suppose there's a lot to explain," said Tru.

"Yes," said Koji.

Trevor was waiting for him at the door. "Come on, don't let Glatz catch us with his damn doors open letting the heat in, or the cool out, whichever."

"Yes," said Koji and he went out after him and paused at the door and looked back when the doors at the other side of the room opened and Mo came back into the room.

"It's arranged. We'll get a ride with my man. He'll be here as soon as."

"I'm going out to smoke," said Koji.

"Great, you asking permission?"

Schleifer again giggled. She was putting her feet into her heels. "Come on ladies, I'll show you something, if you're not too exhausted?"

Tru looked at Koji. "I'm fine."

Koji went outside and Trevor slid the door closed behind them.

"Come with me" said Sofia, "I've something wild to show you," and then she repeated, "Unless you're too exhausted?"

"What kind of thing?" asked Tru.

"You just have to see."

Mo poured herself some coffee. "We've got time."

Tru crunched at her blood-laden shirt. "You think he'd have offered me something fresh to wear."

"We'll get you home soon," said Mo, "Don't worry about it. It's a good look." And she did a rare half-smile.

"Well, if you say so," said Tru. "Come on then, show us this big mystery of yours."

Sofia smiled broadly, put down her cup and walked to the spiral staircase and they followed carrying their cups still and Mo still had that duffel bag slung across her shoulder. Sofia led them to the underside where an alternate staircase went downwards to the level below.

They found themselves stood in a wine cellar with the only light being that allowed down the stairwell behind them. Sofia started moving off into the shadows one way then another.

"I don't know where the lights are. There's a generator somewhere for where I want to show you." She went back towards the stairs, "I'm sure I'll find it all easy enough."

"Don't worry about it," said Mo.

"No you have to see, wait for me."

"No I mean I got a torch." And she had her long torch out of her bag already and had it turned on.

"Just perfect. Come on."

She led them down an aisle of wine racks and then into another and here when Mo whipped her torch around she saw the bottles became more dusted and sparse in number as they progressed along. Then after one more corridor where the racks were nearly entirely empty they entered a large space, and when Mo put her torch around the walls hewn from the cliff interior, and flashed the light along the metal support columns that kept things in order, they saw that the space was near three times larger than the floor-plans of that house above them.

Mo stuck her torch onto Sofia. "What's this supposed to be?"

She took the torch away to give the room another going over and caught a generator at the nearest wall to where they stood, then she followed the cable that came out if it and watched it off the lip of the floor and into a large space dug into it. There was a ladder down, like into a swimming pool but there was no water here. Mo walked to the edge and put the light into the hole.

Tru coming up beside her nearly dropped her cup, stumbled back a step or two and was caught in Sofia's arms. The younger woman held her as they went back to the edge. Mo swished the torch back and forth across the golden figures down there, lined up like a mock Terracotta Army.

"Can you see him?" said Sophia.

Mo returned the words, "See him?"

"It's Herbert Glatz," said Tru.

"What?" said Mo.

They stood there studying the statues, one after the other as Mo rested her beam on them. Each was Herbert Glatz. None were identical in stance but their clothes were always the same. A shirt done up to the neck, high waisted bootcut slacks, and Cuban heels. Sometimes Mo would flash the torch back and forward between them to make sure of the differences in stance and expression, sometimes smiling, sometimes sullen. The poses varied in small ways, here a hand in a front trouser pocket, there one in the other pocket, and there with them both hands crossed in front of him and his feet spread, and so it went on. All facing towards them, all in rows and stood an arms width apart.

Mo broke the stun of the silence that had come on them. "So what the hell is Glatz doing with a basement full of copies of himself? More to the point, what the hell was Lambert David doing with a basement full of Herbert Glatz?"

"It was going to be for his big comeback performance. He still talks about it. And these were going to line the stage."

"Big stage," said Mo.

"Lambert would never allow it to happen, and I think Glatz knew that. And instead he just got carried away. Making one after the other. He still talks about it like it's going to happen. Maybe with Lambert out of the way now it might, who could say?"

Mo continued flashing the torch around. "This Glatz, is he kind of unstable?"

"Such a wasted talent. I think you could say that Lambert sent him a little crazy, with his possessiveness. He never liked anyone else even looking at Herbert. And now Herb's lost five of his best dancing years."

"I get it," said Tru. "David let him indulge in his grand ideas, strung him along, waited until he lost interest in Glatz. I'm sure that would have gotten nasty in time, if he never lost interest. Now they're apart it'll be worse. I bet no one even came down here until last night. Glatz couldn't wait to show off, could he? And I bet Glatz doesn't own a damn thing. I'll bet there's already some boys already on their way to get these trashed."

Mo began traversing along the side of the pit, honing the beam of the torch along the columns. Calling back, her voice echoed off the walls, "If you looked in every Krateran basement, what else do you think you would find? Things you would never guess at."

"It's beautiful," said Tru. Tears came quietly onto her face, unseen in that dark mausoleum. "I can't tell you how jealous I am."

"Of what? Who?" said Mo as she came back to them and then her stomach whined in a high pitch and gurgled loudly. "Well that's the romance killed."

"Not at all," said Tru. "It's perfect."

Sofia took Tru's arm again and started walking her back to the corridors of wine racks.

"Come on, can't believe I brought you down here before talking about food. Let's go and see if we can't find something."

Out into the sun Trevor and Koji had walked with their coffee and to that glass wall looking over the ocean and there stood.

Bachelet had offered Koji a cigarette and Koji had instead taken his pipe from his pocket and packed it and they'd smoked and looked at the sea. Koji had relayed in as best glossed over and fabricated detail as he could muster the events of the night gone. As he spoke he felt like a heavy stone had formed in his stomach. It was as if all his tension and worry were in the confines of that stone, freeing up the rest of him, and his words came easy, the lying about this bizarre event that he had been certain he was to be put in jail for. As he spoke that eventuality seemed impossible.

And it was as Mo had said, that people only feel like any misdemeanour will lead to imprisonment and punishment because the only crimes that are reported are the ones with an outcome. And if something gets big enough on the news they fabricate an outcome, so the cops can make people think they need cops and that they are doing a good job and should have more money.

And the story that they were living now already had its conclusion, that a dog had caused a traffic accident in the dead of the night on a lonely highway. A freak set of events that would make a nice story and that would be that.

What Tru and Koji didn't know was that things were happening all the time with no truthful resolution, that the illusion of being caught by the Bureau, by your words or by your DNA, was by and large a myth to keep the civilians behaving, stop them from shoplifting or fly-tipping or faking their accounts to get away from the taxman. An artifice for the utility of control.

Trevor had listened to the story and then they had smoked quietly for a beat and then he turned suddenly from the sea that they had both watched as they talked. "Hell of a woman, that Tru Beatty."

"Oh yeah? How do you know her?"

"I used to go with her. Real handful those two."

"You dated Tru?"

"That's right. Oh, ten years ago, real history."

"Wow. You seen her since?"

"Around, always when I don't expect it, and this

one probably has to be the best yet. It's like we always end up circling back in together, but like two magnets the wrong way round, you know, like when you try to push them together and they repel each other. Just something that is never supposed to happen. And I just confirmed to her why she was right to ditch me."

"How do you mean?"

"That pendant around her neck, Alice her sister has the other half, like two masks that lock together, something their old man gave them in their teens. After they started looking more like each other that was how you would tell them apart. Some advice for you, never confuse twins when you are dating one of them. Instant death."

"I can imagine. They really look so similar?"

"You don't know them, do you? Famous artists those two, were. They had various names. At the top of their game they went by Al Shahad Mohammad, that was Alice, and . . . " he paused, making sure he was using the right monikers for them, "Shard Al Mohammed, that was Tru. They weren't born identical, but similar looking enough. And they had all these plastic surgeries to finish the job for them. They wore clothes the same, with little differences in the patterns you had to recognise. And those damned pendants of course."

The next draw on his cigarette was long, the blow

of smoke longer. When it was finally done he continued, "And all I did was visit the latrine one day and come back and call Tru by Alice's name and I was done. And the worst thing about that day was that I was slung out immediately and behind me I'd left a stinking shit smell in their house, as my guts were bad from all that drinking we used to do." He looked at Koji and saw the sweat beading on his brow. "Oh, let's get in the shade and sit, you must be hollowed out tramping out there all through the night and then hitting this heat." They moved to an umbrellared table and sat. "I hope you weren't being polite."

"No, I'm alright."

"I don't know you, so maybe I don't know how you normally are. You seem a little spaced out by last night. You need to see a doctor today?"

"No I'm fine. Just very tired. I am sure you can imagine."

"Yeah." Trevor leaned back and put his hands behind his head and rested his eyes and they were quiet a minute.

"What kind of art did she do?"

"Oh, modern art you'd call it. After Shard started to withdraw from public life . . . Tru I mean. After that Alice went solo a while and then there was a controversy because she switched to painting. Tru was always the better painter and they said that she was the one doing the paintings behind the scenes, that it was another performance piece. It kept the papers interested for a while, then the work got called bad by the critics. Some new phase they didn't like. And they said that was Tru sabotaging Alice on purpose."

"Was it bad?"

Trevor shrugged. "I didn't really care for it a lot when it was good, to be honest with you."

"I never heard of those two."

"Not household names, but big in their circles." He laughed. "What a day this is. A house of artistic failures gather here under this roof."

"What's that?"

"Her the artist, me the prodigal concert pianist, him the dancer."

"Glatz?"

"He was in ballet."

"God, I feel embarrassed at my lack of culture. I don't know any of you."

"Culture." Trevor puffed in disdain at the word.

"What is it you do?"

"I'm an engineer."

"There's more culture in engineering than you'll find in the arts pages. I like the idea of that, some practical thing to tackle, without ego."

"I wouldn't say that my field has no egos in it. And I wouldn't say there's not the pressure to impress with the finesse in its application."

"Maybe there's not so much difference in us at all. I bet there's some big names and little ones, and you could say some of them, and me being uncultured in the field, I wouldn't know who you were talking about. We find ourselves staring in a mirror and it is each of us looking back instead of our own selves."

Koji raised his eyebrows. "You must be tired as well, being up all night.

"I'm used to it, but your point is taken. Forgive me for being so wired. Uppers to get me through the night, and then I can say that seeing Tru walking in looking like she's been working an abattoir certainly threw me. And Christ, her seeing I'm running with a critic, of all the girls in the world." He looked at the dark glass of the windows imagining one of the women inside.

"What was it you were saying before, about her being right about having ditched you?"

"Oh, I looked at the pendant on her neck. Like, I got the name right but there was that reflex that made me check I was right about it."

"Oh shit."

"Quite." Trevor threw what was left of his cigarette on the floor and stumped it with his heel. He took Koji's coffee cup. "I get you some more?"

"I think you're right, I'm pretty spaced out. I

haven't even called in to tell anyone where I am. I better do that." He killed his pipe.

The cop Wilford Lebeau pushed a finger under the broad brim of his hat, as if the extra inch of daylight would somehow help in a fathoming of the scene before him. He had been top dog in Blua Haveno since a young age of twenty-six, some ten years.

Not much special happened there, mostly petty domestic stuff. Picking up smugglers was a coast guard problem, practically a military operation, and he just signed off on whatever needed signing for that to go on, but he kept tabs on it, and got paid twice to do so. Twenty- six, someone had discovered, was a perfect age to get a cop corrupted.

With Lambert David finally getting fingered and put away it looked like there was something shifting higher up. And things were shifting down below in the ripples and Lebeau didn't like it. They come for his top donor and who could say what was next? They hadn't started on cops yet, but crusades tended to have their way of getting out of hand.

"Early retirement is starting to look good," said Lebeau. He kicked at some of the spoiled foodstuffs that had spilt from the top of Koji's Barakudo.

"What's that you say?" The old man David Ortiz came away from the car where he'd made a little pile of the best of the salvage on the shaded side, a rough looking figure unshaven and with his dirty little sea captain's hat and white jeans and shirt all grubby the same.

"You checked the hospital?"

"You came out to see me and then I told you about Koji gone missing, and then we came here."

"You remember to get the lighthouse going last night? You remember even getting back there?"

"Yes, and now I feel bad for cursing his name out. He's not the kind of boy to go on a supply run and then get distracted by anything. Not like some that come and help out." He took a hip flask from his front pocket and shook that and then put it back and got another from his arse pocket. "Help out," he ruminated. "That's a joke." He offered the flask over.

Lebeau declined it. "Mhm, well, seems like you have a good gig up there, Davey, some city chumps come and exercise their youthful desire to be a lighthouse keeper, and you make your wage both running the lighthouse and then get all that extra booze money on top."

"It's kids mostly. These younger generations turning up with a knapsack full of old paperbacks written by liars, giving them ideas about life experience. These little berks don't have a clue about actually working for it, they just want it, think it's owed them."

"That who we're looking for now?"

"No, he's one like you said about first, looking for something missing to make up for."

"Well he's this or he's that, you must have a pretty enough pile to get retired out of it by now. Seems like you wouldn't care much he comes back or not."

"Unlike some, my aim isn't to stop working as soon as I'd get the chance for it. Without that you're nothing, it's over. And the day I can't wipe my own arse is the day I jump in the big drink and stay there."

"So what are you putting it all away for?"

"Putting what away? It all goes. Have some respect anyway, looks like the boy's got himself into something bad. Can't say I believe he's got himself out of it either."

"We better get someone to come and clean this up."

"You ever clean up anything yourself, Wil?"

Lebeau let out a breathy allusion at a laugh. Then he started to walk back to his car.

"Come on, let's go and check the hospital. Seems

like both parties got picked up last night and that's where they will have headed." Ortiz wasn't following so he came back. "Don't worry, I'd say your boy's still breathing or I'd have known about that already. That blood out on the road will be a wild dog's blood, and that's what caused the collision. Damned unlucky to be there at that exact wrong moment on an empty road."

"Nope."

"What do you mean, nope?"

"Nope they aint in the hospital."

"They aint in the hospital?"

"Nope."

"So you would like to tell me where they are?"

"Pretty clear there's some tracks leading out the other way into the brush."

"What tracks?"

"Come on." The old man led him past the cars and out a small way and pointed here and there at the ground and at the odd branch of the scraggy bushes pushed out of place, or where a rock had been displaced. "See. Something heavy got carried out this way, to chuck these stones up that way. This ground is hard as hell this time of year, so you won't see much in way of footprints, but it doesn't take much more than looking to see you know I'm right."

"I'm not buying it. It's just those wild dogs. Really

must put in for a budget for someone to come and deal with that, sometime or another."

"Dogs," Ortiz leaned and spat. "Everything happened round here the last decade has been the fault of dogs, wouldn't you say? And the funny thing is, I don't ever remember a single person that ever saw one up close."

"Yeah? Ferocious beasts. You see them you die is why. And then there's old black. With the one red eye. He catches you out after dark and you look in that eye and your whole family dies."

"But not you who looks. So someone would be left to tell about it and nobody ever did. I bet that got you running home well every night you were out playing too late."

"No one would tell, they'd be weighed down by the guilt of it."

"You name me one person you know whose whole family died."

Lebeau looked around the landscape. "I'll put in for a budget anyway."

"Yeah I bet you will."

"So come on, man tracker, you take us to where this heavy load was tooken to. And hurry it, it's starting to cook up out here."

The older man went ahead looking this way and that and stopping occasionally and then going on and

Lebeau strolled behind him, hands in pockets and yawning and thinking about other things but he took notice when they came upon a space in a cranny betwixt a pile of boulders, and found there the shape of a shallow grave and in it a canvas wrapping empty but quite stained with a once bright lifeblood now dark.

"Now, what do you make of that, dog lieutenant?"

"Yes David, it looks like we found your boy."

"We did, then where is he?"

"What we've got is an accident. For some reason, your boy . . . Ishida?"

"Yep, Ishida."

"Ishida for some reason stops out in that dip out on the road. Maybe something dislodged from the supplies he was carrying. He gets out to check, and bam, some arseholes going too fast hit him and his car. Really smashed it. And he's dead right enough, caught in the middle, and those arseholes panic and bury the body. Then they get out on the road and hitch. And I'd say even if we checked up on the owners of that car they'll not be locals. They'll be out of the jurisdiction of Kratera and all its principalities before we get even a sniff."

"You can't call them that without a prince."

"You're a pain, you know that?"

Ortiz knelt to get a look at the grave. "Look at these

marks. That's a pickaxe." He looked about. "Came well prepared. I bet we'll find it hidden up somewhere around here. Hell of a job digging this hard earth. And you care to tell me what he's doing out of the grave?" Their eyes followed the splotches of blood here and there that had dripped and dragged into the earth, trailing away further out into the wilds.

Lebeau adjusted his hat. "I was coming to that."

"Dug up by dogs, right? A lot of effort just for a bit of meat, and looks like they managed to drag him right off to their hideyhole before they started. Funny they should leave all those supplies untouched and come for this instead."

"They smelt the blood."

Ortiz stood and took his hip flask out. "There's one problem."

"Yeah?"

"That grave didn't get scraped out from the top. That grave got undone from below."

"What the hell are you saying now?"

"God spare me, can't you even work that out?" He looked out into the brush and shielded his eyes. "In that state he can't have gotten far. You want to go back and get some bloodhounds recruited, or you want us to start looking ourselves?" He offered the flask again.

The telephone in the reception room was hung up on the wall in an alcove. Koji looked around the place while he held on to its receiver, an odd multi-faceted space that was fairly sparse otherwise. Mostly it was doors.

No answer at the lighthouse. He put the receiver down and flattened out the crumpled piece of paper with the lighthouse's number on it. He took up the receiver again and went to start inputting the number a second time and then that sonorous doorbell tolled from above him. It was loud and he nearly dropped the receiver for it and then hung it up.

Again the bell tolled. He looked to the kitchen door and no-one was coming. He went over to that tall and wide front door and looked at the contraptions for opening it and then partly did so.
Stood on the step was a man in suit jacket with a pale yellow bow tie over a dark shirt, with a yellow

handkerchief in his breast pocket of the suit to match the tie. His face was full-fleshed, and upon it he wore round spectacles and a small sculpted beard that was forked and no moustache and his hair was cut into a flat-top. If he was taken aback by Koji's dishevelled state he showed no evidence of that, instead his little smile pushed his cheeks rounder.

"Good day sir," said the man.

"Good day."

The man put down the doctors bag he was carrying and reached into a jacket front pocket and pulled out a business card. He regarded it himself, swept imaginary dust from the words and then proffered it across.

Koji took the card. The name upon it was long and unusual looking and he imagined the man was waiting for him to mangle the pronunciation. Instead he squinted at the word underneath. "Antiques."

"Antiquities," the man corrected him. "Perhaps the owner of the establishment is present?"

"Perhaps. Depends who you mean. Are they expecting you?"

"Oh, I'm always to be expected."

"Right." Koji looked out at the man's sports car. A navy-blue soft-top Barakudo with the lid down and with the seats in pink. He imagined himself sat in the passenger seat. "I've got one of those myself."

"Yes, an agreeable car. Old but good. You see? Antiques. I drive up in a modern car and already, without realising, perhaps I am mistrusted on some subconscious level. Like I am come to rip them off to surround myself with modern luxuries."

Antiques? Koji took another look at the wording on the business card. "I don't know what to say about that. You could say it looks like you're shelling out on old things like that car in the same way."

"You'd just be saying." The man smiled again.

Koji looked again at the card. "Okay, Mr. Lobo. I'll see if we can get you seen. There was a party, you see? And there's the owner of this place, he's not as such around anymore."

"Oh, of course. I know of those things. An appointment is an appointment."

"Right, what kind of things are you come to look at?" He thought about the artworks in the living area. "Dada stuff?"

The man chuckled and said nothing.

"Right, well, can you hold on a minute?"

The man crossed his hands in front of himself and bowed his head slightly.

"Right," said Koji. The man had stepped up into the space made by the opened doorway when he had handed across the card and Koji didn't know whether to close the door on him, which would be pushing the door to exactly where he stood. As he himself had forced entry into the premises he decided not to. "Antiquities."

He went through the door into the kitchen. The others were all sat at a long high counter that ran the middle of the large kitchen. Stools lined one side of it. Plates now mostly emptied had born devilled eggs and bacon and avocado and toast that Trevor and Sofia had rustled up for themselves and also for these delinquents from out of the wastes, and glasses of fresh juice and water sat beside coffee cups refilled.

They all looked at him from along the counter, Trevor smoking again against the rules of the house at the far end, then Sofia, then Mo, and then Tru closest to him who spoke, "Someone at the door?"
Koji held up the card. "Antiquities. Some weird person." Koji imagined the smiles were all in mockery of him and Sophia came in again with that giggle he only heard directed at himself. He jerked the card towards Tru. "Someone take care of it, will you? Where's that Glatz?"

Tru took the card and read out the name in stops and starts, "Plavia sakun thala Lobo.

"Yes, antiquities. Says he has an appointment. Someone want to go and rouse him up?"

"I'll go and look for him," said Tru. She slipped down from her stool. She turned to Sofia and Trevor.

"Where's his room?"

Sofia pointed in the direction upstairs where his room would be situated. "It's the double doored room at the end of the landing."

"Simple enough."

"Maybe one of those two should go up," said Koji.

Trevor wafted his cigarette at them. "No, be my guest. Herbert doesn't care about formality. The man's off the chain now. He couldn't care less."

Tru went for the door to the main room to then go to that spiral staircase upwards.

Koji went back through the door he had entered through. The man stood exactly how he had left him.

"They're going to get the man of the house to come and see you."The man nodded, almost into a slight bow, and still with that little smile of his.

"I'd offer you a seat inside but it's not my abode, you see?"

"Are you not the gardener?"

Koji regarded his own clothes, dirtied up as they were. He supposed if you did not expect to see dried blood you wouldn't see it. "You think there is one?"

"On the roof."

"Oh, you been here before?"

"First time."

"Right. Well, I better get back to the garden." He held up a thumb and then pushed it slightly at the ceiling. The man nodded again with that little bowing motion and Koji started a retreat back to the kitchen.

"Might I perhaps take some water?" Lobo had out that yellow handkerchief from his pocket and was dabbing at his temples. "It's a terribly hot day already.

A knock came on the double doors at the end of the landing. "Open," called Glatz from the inside and one of the doors opened slowly and Tru stepped in with half her body still concealed behind it.

"Yes yes," said Glatz, "Come in, come in."

He was sat up on four-poster bed, dressed now in a silk shirt done all the way up and some high-waisted slacks. His feet crossed over each other were bare. The papers lay at the foot of the bed, apparently untouched other than his pulling out the comics section, which he was now reading, the back page showing off reprints of Dick Tracy.

"Oh grief, forgive my terrible hospitality, here's me all cleaned up and you still in that bloody shirt."

"There's a fellow downstairs to see you." She looked down at her crusted blouse.

Glatz folded the insert and tossed it aside.

"What now?" He shifted himself over to the side of

the grand bed and swung his feet around and she watched them forage for his loafers that waited there.

"Please, do help yourself to a clean shirt. Most probably might not fit perfectly but I'm sure you can find something." He opened a hand and presented it towards a walk-in wardrobe that still had the door open and the light on inside. "Just don't take my favourite."

"Which one is that?"

"No idea. Now who is it downstairs? The porkoj

She came further into the room, conscious also of her feet still bare and filthy. She offered up the card the man had given Koji.

Glatz came to her and took it and studied it.

"Oh. Yes, I think Lambert said something about this, a man might be coming to visit. With all this that's been going on I can't say I hadn't completely forgotten." He flapped the card up and down, held it to his nose in thought. "No, I can't say I remember what the hell he's after. Alright, I better come down." He walked past her. "Look, my en suite is there, you want to take a shower while you're at it?"

"I have to say, that would be quite something. Don't you have a guest room I could use? Feels awful impressing on you in this way."

"Oh, fill your boots. The guest rooms are probably full of vomit or other effluvia I'd care not to think about." He walked out and left her there. When he was gone she went directly to the newspaper and unfolded it.

David Lambert was the front page news. There he was in the dock, and there was Herbert Glatz in a smaller inset photo being shadowed by a throng of photographers and reporters and the other man pushing them off might be his lawyer but the odd collarless suit said not. She imagined it was that man-help who they had seen leaving in the car, ferrying those last guests back to the city. He was not the figure she was expecting, not much taller than Glatz himself, hard to peg an age to, and his ethnicity too a mystery. She imagined he could fit in to the background in any city on the globe and somehow be mistaken as a local. His thing must be martial arts, to make up for that diminutive stature. Though the photo made him impossible to ignore, he was at once somehow still part of the crowd behind Glatz, his new boss standing lone and vulnerable.

Lambert David himself cut an indomitable figure, at the dock between two cops, cuffed and being led away he was a head higher than each of them. He was smiling in the picture, a mocking kind of a smile, like there was something he knew that no one else had sussed yet. But there he was being sent down for life and probably some longer on top of that.

She flipped open the paper, another double spread on the crime boss felled. And there was this house, at night time. Some sneaky photographer must have hiked in along the coast, hid out there somewhere, making note of all the most prominent guests. A couple more pictures showed some of the biggest names. Actors and artists and performers. No hoodlums, unless they had kept those out of the frame for fear of repercussion, or just because the reading audience wasn't as interested. More like this was Herbert Glatz telling the world he was back, his tenure as a kept man was over. Perhaps this was all intended for Lambert David.

It hurt, if things had been different she'd still be a face of some repute. She'd be in these pictures, her sister on her arm.

She turned the page quickly at the thought, tearing the paper. She'd made page four. Hega Kalson murdered in his Krateran mansion. For some reason they showed his parrot, the caption alluding to this being the only witness. And there in close-up the pendant that belonged to her sister Alice. Kalson had bitten the bullet with it clutched in his hand, having torn it from the neck of his assailant; the laurel-crowned actors mask, long faced and in grimace. She felt to her own neck for the other half, the humoured counterpart.

They'd be in Blua Haveno by now, city pork on tour, arresting Alice, wanting to know where the sister was. Poor Alice. Alice telling them she did not know, and she didn't. Tru had not even had the guts to phone ahead and tell her they'd be coming.

If that damnable dog hadn't been in the road this night before, if she hadn't missed that wretched bus, she'd be there with her now. And their necks would both be bare of pendants, and their agent, the abuser, Hega Kalson, would still be dead by bullets from a tiny pistol. And they would be free. Oh perfect crime gone wrong.

She removed the page from the paper, slipping out the whole sheet that joined pages at the back of the newspaper, folded it, stuck it in her back jeans pocket. It would be a jail cell for Tru before this day would be gone, that felt the certainty. So she'd sure as hell be clean for it. She went to the wardrobe and looked at the shirts.

Glatz came through the doors from the main room and to the reception room and hit the fierce warmth of the day's air coming in and he quickly closed the door behind him. Plaviasakunthala Lobo was stood on the threshold at the main doorway holding a glass of water in one hand and with his chubby digits of the other in his front jacket pocket. A little smile came upon his face.

"Good morning, Mister Glatz."

Glatz came to him and ushered him in and closed the door to the outside. "I can't believe they left you standing there in this heat."

"Oh I'm quite fine. Your gardener brought me some chilled water." He held up the glass.

"I see." He held up the card Tru had given him. "Doctor Plaviathakunsala Lobo PhD."

"—sakunthala."

Glatz looked again at the spelling. "That's you."

"That is myself."

"You care to tell me what business you've driven out here upon? I mean, I trust you read the newspapers? I trust you realise this is not a great day to be doing business upon?"

"Yes, I quite understand. Your benefactor, Mister Lambert David, had arranged this meeting some time ago, and he insisted that whatever happened to him between then and now, that I should come to the house and talk with his successor."

"He did, huh? Well I'm not his successor."

"You are Herbert Glatz."

"Did he call me his successor? I live in his house. This is still his property. His businesses are quite something apart from me."

"I would say you are the new rightful occupant of this villa?"

"It's debatable. You want to check that with my lawyers and the City lawyers?"

Lobo smiled. "You are a very open man in this private matters. Mister David did warn me about that."

"He did? He told you a lot it seems, and yet here's me having never heard of you."

"Oh, really he didn't tell me too much, just enough to facilitate business."

Glatz stood quietly considering this man. His brow

told the man he was doing this and the man waited.

"Let's go in my study here, and maybe we can get this sorted, I hope with some expediency. It's been quite the long night."

Koji opened the door to the toilet and came out to the sound of flushing and hurriedly closed the door in his wake. He thought the design poor, to put the lavatory in the nose of these other doorways, but the fierceness of the fans he could hear going on the other side of that now closed door told him that someone else may have had the same thoughts.

"Ah, my good gardener," said Glatz. "It seems you've stayed on beyond your morning shift."

"Yes, just waiting for our ride."

"Good good." He took the glass from Lobo and gave it to Koji. "We'll be in my study here. If you could be so good to bring in some coffee for us while we talk business?"

"Yes, of course."

"Good good. And tell that piano player not to smoke in my kitchens." Glatz went to the door to the study and opened it and went in and turned on a lamp on a desk and went around it and sat in a chair. "Do come in, Doctor."

On the way to picking up his bag from the floor Lobo gave Koji that little nod-bow of his again and Koji wondered if Lobo saved it for him only. He watched the man go into the study, saw inside briefly as this visitor closed the door behind himself, at walls that carried what looked mostly to be tomes of law on the shelves there.

Koji went through to the kitchens. The three still there were quiet, the conversation all dried up. Mo and Sofia sat at that thin high counter and Trevor was piling up dirtied plates by the large sink with a tea towel over his shoulder but he wasn't making any moves to actually do any washing up.

To Mo Koji said, "Why didn't you come to the door? Could have been our lift."

"It was too fast. Couldn't have been him."

"How long do you think it's going to be?"

Mo looked at her watch. "Not so long."

"Twenty minutes? Half an hour."

She shrugged softly. "I guess."

"Uh huh. Glatz wants some coffee for that visitor of his."

The two women looked at him and said nothing about that. Trevor turned from the sink and rested against it. "Just take that pot there, it's still enough warm." He took his cigarettes out again.

Koji ignored relaying the message from Glatz and went and took the pot and a couple of fresh cups in the other hand and went back out, pushing backwards the swing door. He went to the study and tapped and awkwardly got the handle open and went in and the men carried on talking.

Glatz leaned back in his chair, tooling with a letter opener that was shaped like a sabre with a hand guard that would permit one finger behind it. He gesticulated with it as he spoke. "If I remember correctly, Lambert said it was the clock you were after. Now you're talking about wine. I can't say I was paying him a lot of attention, what with everything that's been going on. I'm pretty certain it was that Bauhaus clock."

"He may have mentioned time, but not in regards to your clock, mister Glatz."

Koji set down the pot and cups and Lobo did that annoying little nod. He was now entirely sure that Lobo reserved it for him only. He didn't go so far as to pour for them and he stood there a beat. Without acknowledgment from Glatz he wasn't ready to walk out again, but he was also aware of the jeopardy of being dismissed like a worker if he stood much longer and so he left.

He left the door open and Glatz watched him as he spoke. "Well, Doctor Lobo, I can't say the timing is the best in the world." He saw Koji hesitate at the door to the kitchen and turn and decide to go through to the main room of the house. "But if you drove all the way down here for this?" He stood and still looked at the two doors Koji had left open, breaking the seal on the air-con from the big room, "Let's go and see if we've got what you're looking for."

Lobo came out after him and Glatz closed the door to the study and they went into the main room. Koji was going back out of the sliding glass door to the swimming pool area. As Glatz closed the doors behind him he was readying to berate Koji for leaving the outer door open also but Koji was already sliding it to shut.

They went to the spiral staircase and went down. At the bottom Glatz found the light switches that Sofia had not. Bare lightbulbs came on, strung up intermittently along the aisles formed by the wine racks, suspended in cones that made isolated circles on the floor. Glatz went ahead, vanishing and appearing into those stark bubbles of light as they zig-zagged the path that took them back further through the collection.

"It's ordered by date," said Glatz. "And you want the oldest." They came on the last row. One wall of wine away from entering the cavern of golden Glatzi. The lights stopped in this aisle and the statues stayed in darkness in the pit beyond, their own lighting rigged to that generator now off.

Glatz studied the shelf, then looked around for and found the small stool that had one side of laddered slats, and climbed up them and reached.

"Do be careful, mister Glatz. I really don't think you know how valuable is the item."

Glatz lifted down a bottle and passed it to Lobo and then took another and he came down and Glatz dusted his bottle with his hands, sending a mote cloud into the nearest cone of light which they stepped into and both set to regarding the bottles. Lobo had his bag put down and his handkerchief from his chest pocket and wiped down his own bottle as Glatz lifted his up to the light, the glass a purplish hue. "So this is where Lambert was storing all of his wealth?"

From somewhere Lobo had produced a monocle of the like you'd expect from a person verifying a jewel authentic. He placed the monocle over his eye and held up the bottle and studied the label with its century old illustration, a skyline with mostly squared off buildings, and above it a great meteor hurtling earthward from above. Glatz was impelled to study the identical label on the bottle in his own hands.

Lobo took off the monocle and did a smile that showed where it had left a divet in the top of his cheek. "A city of Brutal inclination. The city's mayor had, of a hundred years past, been the first in a long line of fervent idealists, nepotism replacing each that has come since with a kindred spirit all down the line, a cabal that had hijacked those rich farmlands, built that city from scratch in the great impact crater, gouged out, they said, by a great artefact that had fallen there some many thousands of years ago."

"Where are you from yourself, Doctor Lobo?"

Lobo continued as if the question had not been asked, "What is it about the city of Kratera that makes impossible cellular phones, that makes impossible any kind of radio waves? The artefact, they say. The only mayor that had promised to dig and get that mystery solved didn't last long. There is in that city a cultist elite who want things to stay as they are. How terrible it would be to find a banal answer to the great mystery that gave that place its soul. And these people make up my customer base."

Glatz sat down upon those small steps. He was right to know this bore was not finished and so Lobo continued:

"The soul was twisted. It had the same lack of depth as the new cultures of the North Americas, or the antipodes, something missing that only a long history could provide. Back here on the old continent, the displacement of the original farmers and caretakers of this land had been many degrees less violent than the horrors faced by those other Indigenous peoples, nonetheless there was a stain just the same."

Lobo turned the bottle in his hands, regarding the skyline on the label. "This city, even now a century old and well established, still regarded as new, like a mini state of its own, had attracted peoples from all over the world, welcomed by the great founder, first mayor Meyer. To build and settle, to shirk off their old cultures and become an example of what the integration of peoples could really achieve. And by and large it had been a success until the digital age, the failure of mobile communications setting it further and further afield as the years progressed. Internet cafes still rule there. And so too crime and deviance. They poured in from all over, a new type, those running from something, or those looking for something, or to take advantage of those who tried."

"Yeah, do go on."

"Kratera had become the number one destination for thrill seekers. The laws there somewhat grey in many matters that suited that overclass. It had been designed as something of a new socialist beginning, but the spirit of Man, the very thing that makes men Man, will always desire a hierarchical arrangement. And the old class, the old families who had invested the most to get the city built, rose to the top, became richer still. The police became more authoritarian, and simultaneously corrupted. The underground societies at either end of the scale burgeoned."

"Is this going somewhere special, Doctor?" He said 'doctor' with some small edge to the word, some disdain perhaps at this man's hazy area of expertise. Glatz stood up. He had a creeping sense that by letting this man into his house a grave error had here been committed. After a party it was the perfect moment. His guard was down. He started to wonder also about those three that had walked out of the scrublands like a holy trio on pilgrimage. He felt the effort of the past weeks and the long night coming down on him, slowing his cogs.

Lobo ignored him. "The founders had imagined a city that would be the envy of the world. In those early days there were strict rules as to who could come. Jobs were allotted in a quota to be filled, to later be handed over to their children, and from that moment it was doomed to fail, to ignore the organic in pursuit of ideology, was like pushing the barrel towards the waterfall. Any city that became the envy of the Nazis could only ever end as a city riven with corruption. What started as the most controlled situation the world had ever seen, the most bald grab for a Utopia, was inversely now the freest. A Utopia for some but not all and not many. For each traveller who enters its gates it is the best city in the world, and for many it can quite soon become the worst."

"It was a city like any other," said Glatz, "If it was your city, it would have been yours."

"Yes, that is the quote." Lobo held up the bottle

again and saw the same phrase printed in a banner on the label but in Esperanto, the failed language chosen for that new state. "I apologise, I can see my talking has disturbed you."

"I'll admit I'm lost about what you are trying to teach me. You're making some kind of assertion about my character, or that of Lambert's, and frankly, I don't like the cut of your jib, Mister Lobo."

"You must forgive me. I just like to talk. It fascinates me, socialism, utopianism, krateranism, all of these attempts to subvert the natural order of things. And to answer your question, I am not a native Krateran."

"And for you, is it the worst city or the best?"

"But of course the best. Where else could I sell a city's history to its own peoples at such costs?"

Glatz smiled at that. "It's quite the racket. The price you agreed for these two bottles with Lambert. What's the markup for the sell on?"

"Now now, let's not get into the vulgar details."

"Why not? It would suit the vulgarity of the city you have so pained to outline for me, as if I never heard of the place. I don't understand your game, Mister Lobo, but I do know that I have been awake a long night and am really not best in a position to fathom it, or even to much have an interest in it. I can't say I would have any even if I were at my best. So shall we conclude this business?"

"That was quite the echo." Lobo went to the wine rack, tried to peep through some of the gaps at the dark cavern beyond.

"Yes, it's a natural cave in the rock."

"Oh? Not susceptible to collapse I hope? And with all this wealth on your shelves down here, you'd do well to make sure there's no other entrance."

"Sure. Why not? Everyone wants to get in here and rob us, or murder us in our beds. If any of Lambert's rivals wanted us out of the picture they could just easily send enough brutes through the front door."

"Oh it seems that's been taken care of quite another way by the City itself. Do you suspect his enemies in business were behind the manoeuvres?" " I couldn't care less anymore. The old fascist set for all I know."

"His old associates then?"

"This is ridiculous, I just let a man in to buy two bottles of wine. A man I never met before. Lambert just got sent down for the rest of his breathing days, and yet he's taken the time to arrange the sale of two bottles of wine. Just what exactly is going on here, Lobo?"

Lobo laughed again. "Here, a second letter." He reached into his jacket and took out an envelope. He passed it across. Glatz put down the bottle onto the stool and then stuck a pinky finger under the flap and tore open the envelope and took out the paper and studied it, studied the stamps of certification and the arranged value of a single bottle of vintage Krateran.

"Holier Christ," said Glatz. "That amount?" His eyes went up to the bottle Lobo held, as if by staring into it hard enough its value would reveal itself.

"Especially manufactured for that party that signalled the official opening of Kratera. Every new citizen was invited, each in their allotted roles for this new city marked out on a little certificate. Each certificate exchanged for one of these bottles. And how many exactly, do you think remained undrunk? It was considered unpatriotic to the new endeavour not to partake, even the children. Like a sacrament. A clever move. Dividing your populace into those who had gorged, had taken the communal blood inside them, and all other outsiders, who were not touched by holy sacrament. How to put a value on holy remnants? You see, whatever may have happened personally between yourself and Lambert David, and knowing that the City is coming to claim all of his assets, it looks like he wanted you to live out your life in some comfort."

Glatz folded the letter, replaced it into its envelope and picked up the other bottle with some care. "That old dog. This whole time it was here. It's a miracle it got through this night untouched. I opened the cellar and let the guests have at it."

"And here is the cheque awaiting my signature." He produced the cheque from his top pocket where his handkerchief had been and unfolded it and held it up so that Glatz could read off the designated amount for two bottles of Krateran. "Yes, it is less than the letter stated, but I must take my cut, you see? And so, the vulgar details."

"Fine. Just fine."

"Shall we return to your study to conclude our business?"

"Let's go outside, get the gardener to witness."

Fresh from the shower and now dressed in a red silk shirt, Tru slid the door open to the balcony. She walked around the curve of the upper floor to where she was getting a look at the inland scenery, felt the blaring sun instantly sucking at her hair still wet. The shirt had some intricate pattern more obvious in the strong light, and she'd have no idea about what those patterns were of if you'd asked her. Dragons, flowers, whatever. She wore a pair of his slacks but they were too short so she'd put a couple of rolls into the legs to make it less obvious.

She thought of that newspaper, at those scum reporters who had been hiding out there to picture the guests arriving, to pap them, to fill up some empty column space. She thought about Sofia Schleifer, who was of that world. A critic, but still part of the machinery, machinery that Tru had fallen outside of in recent years, had been absent from until she'd unloaded that pistol into Hega Kalson, and had delighted to watch the surprise as consecutive slugs had torn into his organs, and with a final hole in his cheek she had enjoyed to watch his cognition fade out of the world.

She threw her head back and laughed one of her full bodied laughs. The kind that took people off guard, thrilled or horrified them every time she did it. The most impressive headline the twins had ever hit the papers with and it was bumped to second story by the owner of this very house she found herself in

She moved to go back inside, stopped herself and looked back to see the small rifling of dust out there on the main highway some distance away, but too much dust for the highway. The car had turned off and was making its approach, too soon to be Herbert Glatz's bodyguard back from Kratera.

On turning back to look at the car, a second detail from that landscape had made a delayed entrance into her thought; a flash, a glint. Where had it been? She pulled out the memory and replayed it. A hallucination brought on by her exhaustion? No, she had seen it, something close, some surface out there that had broadcast a reflected beam of that ferocious star straight into her retina. The print of it was still bleached onto her inner eye and she knew where to look. Down there by that tree that crested a small natural ridge in the landscape. She leant on the balcony and looked there and saw naught. And then her mind was back in the newspaper. She was seeing that shot of Lambert David's house, this house, and those film stars and assorted hobnobs, and she saw in reverse where they had been pictured from, and that one and only place it would have been possible to picture the house from that close and stay unseen.

"You sons of bitches."

She took one more look at the dust making its way to the house, someone not scared to toe it. That would be Mo's man. And then she went back inside. Perhaps by association with the David residence they'd tomorrow make front page after all.

By the poolside the three men, Glatz, Lobo, and Koji Ishida, sat beneath the shade of an umbrellared table. Koji out there by himself smoking his pipe, at the same seat he'd previously taken beside Trevor, had been joined by the two men wielding their two bottles now placed upon the table.

Koji was stood now, leant over and studying the piece of paper he was being asked to sign, and then he put his pipe into his mouth and took the man Lobo's fountain pen and signed and handed it back across the table and sat back in his chair putting the lid back onto the pen.

"Very good, Mister Ishida." Lobo slid the second copy towards him.

He leaned and squinted hard at it, read it cursorily, too embarrassed to talk of his lost glasses and his inability to make out much of it.

"The same?"

"The same."

He undid the pen and signed and slid back the paper and re-lidded the pen and handed that over also.

"Is this the natural order of things, doctor?" asked Glatz, "El capitalismo?" He put a hand on Koji's arm. "That's just splendid, Mister Ishida. Thank you for bearing witness. And don't think I won't let you enjoy some of this bounty for the taking part. But probably best don't tell your companions. The jealousy. Unless you're the sharing type as well of course."

"No no, I couldn't accept that." He had not been able to make out the figures involved but the number looked long.

"No no, I must insist."

Lobo smiled. "Curious isn't it, Mister Ishida. One hundred years in the waiting. And your own predecessors quite living their own lives on another continent, and one day the fruit of their progeny will come into contact with a bottle of wine, and so the gardener gets his bonus."

Koji went to adjust his glasses out of a habit. "My forebears were right here. They were founding Kraterans."

Glatz laughed. "Then they had their own bottle of the plonk."

"Oh, original tree shapers," said Lobo. "Mister

Ishida, if only they had the sense of Lambert David's forefathers not to pop the cork."

"That would have seemed like the sensible thing. My ancestors you couldn't call rogues. Being a gardener suits me just fine. What's more to want? Sleeping you take up one tatami mat, awake, a half." He held up his fist. "A fistful of rice is all your belly can hold."

Lobo did his irritating nod. "Very nice. Is that yours?"

"You'd like to hear that I took it from a manga."

Lobo chuckled. "Well, all the same, by your families stalwart approach to life you have quite by chance come to be in this right place at this right time. And so to conclude the business I will carry out the letter of my instruction by Mister Lambert as promised."

He took up his doctors bag and put it on his knees and opened it and put in one of the bottles and the signed papers. He he took out a Swiss army knife. Then he put his bag aside on the floor and took up the other bottle and put it between his knees, and opened the corkscrew.

Glatz's hands flew up and hung in the air. "What are you doing? Are you entirely crazed, man?"

Lobo plunged the curled metal into the cork of the bottle and started to twist it home. "When I agree to carry out my duties, I must carry through. Perhaps you think we could have saved this one bottle and sold it and taken the money, and our benefactor would be beyond our worries, so safely locked up in the jails."

"Yes perhaps. Of course perhaps."

"These are the instructions." He tugged out the cork and the pop of it rang loud around the space. He lifted the corkscrew and wafted the cork under his nose. "When last did anyone bear this scent?" He held it towards Koji.

Koji refrained from leaning towards it. He held up his hand. "A gardener wouldn't know one wine from another. Perhaps a rice wine would have been better."

Lobo put the opened bottle on the table and placed the Swiss army knife back inside his bag, cork still attached, and then took out three crystalline tumblers. "I understand that you may have had a heavy night, Mister Glatz, but I am sure one small sup of this wine would not push you over an edge. Such is the request of the boss. From this day forward you are declared an independent of him. Now you have your own wealth."

They both looked at Herbert Glatz for his reaction and at that moment they heard faintly he bell tolling to tell of an arrival at the house.

"Now who the hell is this?" said Glatz.

"You want me to go again?" said Koji. "Could be

Mo's fellow come to pick us up."

"Let someone else check. Here, partake." Glatz picked up the bottle as Koji was standing. He poured into one of the glasses, a red rich and deep.

Koji covered his hand over the closest glass.

"Please excuse me, you see, I am a teetotal."

Glatz poured into Lobo's glass. "Oh come on. Don't be a stiff." He held the bottle ready to pour. Koji lifted his hand but the door to the house slid open and there stood Tru in Glatz's clothes and they looked to her.

"He's here. Our ride is here."

Koji stood. "Well, if you'll excuse me. It's been splendid."

"Thanks Ishida," said Glatz. "Please, do go carefully from now on."

"Yes. Thank you."

Tru came out to them. She presented her hands and dipped a foot to show the clothes she had taken.

"I'll get these back to you."

Glatz wafted a hand. "Ah forget it." He put down the bottle and got up and took both her hands in his. "I've been happy to help. Who knows, perhaps our paths will meet again. If I recall correctly we once met previously? I didn't recognise you at first. I believe we know many of the same people."

"Perhaps so. That would be nice. Goodbye." She looked to Koji and they both walked away and excluded Lobo from the farewells. They heard glasses clinked as they left and the two men saying 'salutoj.'

In the reception room they found Mo standing in the doorway in what looked like a heated discussion with a man, short haired and with a thin moustache and with a similar dress sense to Mo and they looked of a piece.

"This is Rahul."

Rahul Gupta looked Koji over. "This is who caused us the grief?" Stunned, Koji had no comeback. Rahul took up the slack, "I had the scanner on all the way in here and I can tell you they're out looking for you."

"Not Mo or Tru?"

"Not for being in the wreck," said Rahul. "That's not our biggest problem right now." He walked out and towards his car and the others followed out of the door.

Tru squatted to put her sandals back on that sat where she'd left them by the steps. Koji waited with her. The door to the house behind him gaping and spewing cooled air.

"What's he talking about?" he asked.

"One, the Glatz party got papped."

"It got what?"

"Paparazzi. Out there by that tree. Big party, lot of big names, the papers like that kind of thing, gets them to draw out the Lambert David scandal."

"So what?"

"Well guess what? Someone put in the long shift."

"What?"

Tru finished up getting her shoes on and stood.

"They're still out there. They watched us in, they took our pictures."

"How soon is that a problem? I can't be talking to the cops right now. I'm fried. Can you even remember our dog story? We should practice it over again."

"I said that was problem one. You want to hear the second?"

"They found him?"

"Oh in a sense. In another not."

"What?"

"They found an empty grave."

"What?"

"We buried a man alive, Koji."

"No we didn't."

"Yes, yes we did."

"How?"

"You remember putting in much grit to dig that hard ground very deep?" She laughed.

Mo and Rahul over by the car talking low but aggressively to each other stopped and looked over at them and then got back to their conference.

Koji sat on the steps. "How is that funny, Tru?"

"The whole thing is funny, isn't it?"

"I can't believe I let you two convince me to walk out of there. We should have just sat tight, waited for the cops. They were always going to find me, it's my car. It was an accident. What was I thinking? Now what do we do?"

"I need to be with my sister."

"Let's think on the way down to Blua Haveno." They watched as Rahul started walking to the tree. "What's this now?"

Mo pulled on Rahul's arm but he shook it off and continued marching out there. Mo went and got in the car.

Tru set off after Rahul. "This I want to see."

"Maybe we shouldn't get involved?"

Tru carried on after Rahul and Koji went after her. When they caught up Rahul stood with an arm outstretched onto the trunk of the tree. There was the reporter doing up his rucksack as if readying to leave and the photographer stood with her hands on her hips and her camera hanging down from around her neck.

Rahul sniffed at the air. "I smell rats."

"Come on Lyn, let's get going." The reporter slung his rucksack up on his back and stood up. He was half-turned away from Rahul, ready to head out south the way they'd come in along the cliff.

"Who are you supposed to be?" said the photographer.

The reporter's head went down. "Leave it."

"You shut up," said Rahul. "The woman's got heavier stones than you have. Not even the guts to face up to being the rat you are."

"We've got our job," said the photographer, "You've got yours. We're done. So we'll be on our way."

"Yeah you do that." Rahul looked up at the lowest branches of the tree, touched upon one then another, giving each a gentle pull to gauge resistance, and that second dry branch he pulled on harder and snapped it away. They watched as he turned it in his hands clearing smaller branches.

The reporter had started slowly walking away, made a few quicker steps and stumbled when Rahul jumped down to their level. Rahul was on him fast, pulling him up by his rucksack so he looked like a puppet.

"Come here you rat fuck."

The photographer came in and Rahul with the hand

carrying the stick shoved at her and she batted at his arm. As she pushed his arm away he then took the stick and pushed it under the reporter's nose longwise, one hand still controlling him by his backpack.

"You want me to splat this rat then you keep on grabbing at me, woman."

She stepped back. "Alright, you want to play it that way." She took the camera up and started taking photos. Rahul pushed the stick harder and the reporter had his arms on the stick trying to push it down as it ground at that hard part that divided his nostrils, and he moaned at the pain of that.

Koji and Tru looked on from the top of the ridge, unmoving, untalking, spectral witnesses.

Rahul let the stick come down and the reporter put his hands to his nose and checked them for bleeding. As his hands came down Rahul brought the stick up again and put one end into one of his nostrils and pushed up and you could see one side of his nose flaring. The reporter yelled out a guttural noise and grabbed at the stick. The shutter noises stopped and the photographer came in with her paws up in a way that told of some boxing training in her past and round-housed Rahul into the side of his head.

He paused at the surprise of that and the reporter took the moment to pull the branch down and out of his nose.

Rahul slung the reporter by the backpack and he fell. He turned on the photographer who backed off a couple of steps but with her hands still up.

"Let it go man. Like I said, just doing our job. Now you have to make it unlawful."

"Unlawful? You rat finks come sniffing around here spying like this? That's in the law? If that's in the law, what kind of law is that?"

"This is off their property, we can do what we want here."

"No, I don't think so."

"Doesn't matter what you think."

"Alright let's make a deal, you give me the film that has my friends in it, and we'll call it quits."

"Film? Where you from? The nineties?"

"Jesus Christ, Lyn," said the reporter muffled, his hands around his nose with a little blood coming between the fingers. "Just give it to him. Who cares about who these people are?"

"See, your boy got the message. Now why can't you?"

She started to shake her head but the stick came in fast and whipped across her face. She yelled in pain at that, went to holding with both hands the welt that had slashed some blood up there. Rahul came in, grabbed at the camera.

She went submissive as he yanked it up over her head and then he shoved her with it in his hand, staggered her back a few paces.

"See, you never had to lose a camera over it. Now you pissed me off. He started walking towards the cliff edge and as he walked started swinging the camera by its strap. "See, I'll even give you a chance, because I like your spunk."

He hurled it and they all watched it arc in the air and go out and down beyond the edge of the cliff and the rocks below were so far that they would not hear it bashing apart there out of their sight.

"You get down there and find that and I'll let you have your pictures." He walked away back to the ridge, kicking some dust at the reporter as he passed, and then he climbed back up and looked at Tru and Koji stood there immobile and then he walked back to the car and Mo got out as he approached.

To Tru Koji said, "Great, now we get to be witnesses for that too?"

"In the bigger picture, Koji, that's the least of your worries."

"You think?" He trailed her back to Rahul's car.

Rahul went to get in the driver's side. Mo came to them. "Alright, we done you two a favour, but things have changed now, we've got that friend of ours still walking around out there. Chances are he didn't get very far, probably croaked for real. But it still changes things."

"I swear he was dead," said Koji. "He was so quiet. He wasn't breathing, was he?"

Tru folded her arms. "You tell me how else a person stays alive if they don't breathe? We were sloppy."

"Sloppy?" said Koji going to adjust his absent glasses. "Like we didn't finish him off sloppy?"

"He must have been still ticking over," said Mo. "Like one of those frogs you put in the freezer or whatever. It's not properly dead, just slowed right down, asleep."

"And maybe there was like an air bubble in the canvas we buried him in," said Tru, "You know, like when a boat upturns and you can go underneath."

"I can't believe this has happened," said Koji.

"Boring," said Tru.

"It's going to be more boring when we talk to the cops about it."

"You speak for yourselves," said Mo. "Me and Rahul are splitting. You want to talk to the cops, go for it. My experience it's only a matter of time with squares like you, Koji."

"That's not fair. We helped you out last night just as much as the other way around. I'd say it's looking like more so. Your fellow there just made things even harder for us by assaulting those two poor bastards over there."

"Poor bastards?" said Tru. "Those people are scum."

"They're people though, and people don't usually walk away quite so easily after they get sticks rammed up their schnoz holes. Mo and Rahul are going to be just fine, they'll ride off, switch cars, slip over a border or whatever. You and me, Tru? We'll still be right here."

Tru shrugged. "It doesn't matter for me anymore."

They all three went quiet a moment and then Mo said, "Listen, me and Rahul, we're going now. We're not giving you your ride to Blua Haveno like you want. We're going back through Kratera. So, sorry, we won't get you your ride. Looks like you're stuck here some longer." She held her hand out for Koji and he looked at it and then he shook it. "Don't worry, I don't think you're a square. I'm just embarrassed. I had you two picked the moment we met."

"What a way to meet." He took his hand away, "What a way."

Mo went to shake Tru's hand. And Tru clasped it and said, "Wish we could have met in another way."

"We wouldn't have."

"I know. Listen, why don't you give those two in there who made us breakfast that ride to the city? Rahul probably not up for that?"

Mo looked at the car as if doing so would tell the answer. "Maybe we can get them some of the way at least, unless they want to carry on and wait for Glatz' driver to come back."

"Alright, I'll go and ask. Give us a minute."

"Hurry it. We need to move on. Rahul will already be pissing blood at me."

Mo turned and went back to the car and then Tru and Koji went back into the house, leaving again that front door open to the heat.

"Would you consider it to be a beautiful view?" Plaviasakunthala Lobo looked out at the sea. "Why is it do you think that people take photographs when they are looking at a sea or a sunset or beautifully lit clouds? The photos never compare to what you are looking at with the naked eye, not unless photography is your trade, and then it is so often a matter of deceit, of tweaking, of hyping what was there to see, and so now you have captured an unreality."

He smiled and waited for a response from Glatz but there was none so he continued, "If you close your eyes. In five minutes, two, even one, can you remember those lovely cloud formations? Are they still beautiful? How lovely for all the people to stand in front of a thing and say how splendid it is. So curious how often they have to say those words, as if by leaving it unsaid would put it into doubt. And it is to be doubted. There is no beauty in inconstancy."

He leaned to his bag and picked out the unopened bottle of Krateran.

"Here is beauty. Value in something that does not change from one moment to the next. Which in an instant could be squandered." He held it out over the wooden decking, feinted as if he was dropping it and then held it firm again. He put it back into his bag. He sat and looked at Herbert Glatz and Glatz seemed vacant and unresponsive.

"Ah good. The poison is working."

Glatz's glazed eyes focussed for a moment and he went to talk but only a voiceless breathy sound came from down inside his chest. On his brow he managed a quizzical frown.

Lobo leaned over and took one of Glatz's limp wrists and felt the pulse and that turned into holding his hand.

"You may wonder what antiquities I specialise in, and no it is not bottles of wine. It is in poisons. Let me just explain and then my business will be fully completed. It was one of the conditions of the deal. Your benefactor Lambert David. You did so think that you might be free of him now, and that would include his wealth. But no, with this arrangement you stay wealthy, but you stay his person. It seems his love for you is all encompassing, and if he cannot any longer have access to you physically then he must act and, let us say, alter your physicality."

He played with Glatz's fingers as he talked, watched as those numb digits failed to push his own away. "There will be no comeback show for you, Mister Glatz. He would not have you gazed upon by others. Already you know his attentiveness to quashing as much footage of your performances as he could get his hands upon. You could call it jealousy, or true passion, and I call it merely my duty to carry out. Your little army of golden effigies will be melted down. No one will see them. I am sure already you have scuppered Lambert David's intentions with your surprise party of the last night, your first taste of freedom so you might describe it as."

He let go of Glatz's fingers and sat back in his chair. "I am quite certain you wouldn't have been able to keep that spectacle in your basement cavern a private matter. It's been a long time you working on them and having no audience. A man such as yourself lives for an audience, the one thing this relationship with Lambert David has extinguished in the old sense. Who is your audience now? Those studying the column inches of the newspapers? A grainy photo here and there through a car window?"

The door to the house slid open and Trevor and Sophia came out. She had her handbag on her shoulder and he had his suit jacket slung over his.

"Thank you for your hospitality, Herbert," said Sophia without coming over to them. "It's been splendid."

"We've got a lift back to town," said Trevor. He held up an envelope that had his payment inside. "I hope you'll think of me next time you have a little get together up here."

Glatz managed to raise his hand off the table. They took that for a farewell in a dismissive kind of way and then left and closed the door.

"Oh a pity. How blind people can be at what is apparent right in front of them. People see what they look for, not what is actually there." Lobo cast a hand again at the ocean view. "This isn't even for our eyes to see. What we see is information crammed back into our little monkey heads and then projected out again based on everything we already knew of the world. We live in our fantasies."

He smiled again at Glatz, his head tilted and considering. "You disliked me from the out. You disliked the way I talk. What a terrible torture it must be to sit there and be listening to me now without recourse. If only those two had known that I have the antidote in my bag, that if taken within sixty three minutes the damage would be almost entirely reversed."

Lobo took the small bottle from his bag and placed

it on the table and watched Glatz's fingers straining for it, watched the trickling sweat pour over the veins bulging at his temples. He moved the bottle further from Glatz's hand, a few inches, impossibly far.

He took up and raised his own glass. "Salutoj." He drank and put it down again. "The poison will not work on me. The poison was upon the rim of your glass. A poison that is ancient, that will be detectable, that will match a rare toxin found in seafood. Something similar to that used in the Caribbean, to so comatise a victim, to have him dug up later and zombified. Well, at least you won't be cleaning anyone's toilet as a mindless slave, that at least will not change."

He gestured at the platter that Tru had spilt earlier.

"Convenient. A coincidence you might say? How lucky I chose a poison that matches something at the scene of the crime. Oh but I do my homework. No coincidence. This spread you put on, that might be their first understanding of what has happened to you. In time you will be trained to communicate via your eyes, they will build a special robot for you. You will not have the strength required to get up, or to talk, or to wield a knife to cut your veins. Without the antidote you'll become fully comatose and sadly it's fifty fifty as to how much of your present cognition will live on out the other side."

Lobo sighed well at that and looked at the ocean

"He wanted me to tell you, before your mind might be gone forever, that it was your keeper Lambert David behind this. That was not my choice, but I always carry out my duty. How could you have stopped this? Well, your instant party was not a good idea. That was the trigger, and that set things into play. I suppose he was considering not going through with this, that you might have taken heed of his wishes and instructions about how to comport yourself in his absence. Perhaps after some months his jealousies would subside, he might find himself a new toy behind bars for his affections. Which I am certain will come to pass. Too late." He lifted his glass to the light. "Not bad. I've had better." He stood and picked up his bag.

He went to walk away and then stopped and reached into Glatz's shirt pocket and took out his own calling card and placed it back in one of his own, "Good day sir. Your man help will be back soon enough so I understand. Lawva Carrauza. Don't worry, your benefactor has instructed him to stay in your service. Such painful duties he now has, to look after you in your coming state. Yes I do think there could have been another way out, if you had waited, if you had stayed discreet. I would have come and bought the Krateran from you, and your master would have changed his mind about this final deed, and you would have been both a free and a rich man. You might have danced again. I did see you once before. I was there at your last show. Like gazing upon a so called beautiful view, I took no pleasure in that which is ephemeral. My delight is in watching the theatre of it, to bask in the ridiculous. You might want to use that newfound wealth of yours, make use of it to employ me to exact some revenge on the man who has made your body a prison. Unfortunately I cannot. If I did so my reputation would be in ruins. Perhaps I will come and see you again after I am retired, though I can't yet say when that would be."

He stood a moment longer with his doctors bag in both hands in front of him and raised it slightly.

"Greedy, you might say. I could now live happily enough on the wealth from this one job alone. I would say to you that it's not really about the money. A man's work is his work." He was quiet a moment and looked at the view again, and whatever he was considering in that moment would be left unsaid. "I will not be so crass as to say farewell, so I will leave it at a goodbye. Goodbye Mister Glatz."

He turned at that, walking back to the house with Glatz's eyes burning him down while a puddle of piss formed underneath the chair where he would remain sat until taken away.

When Lobo was gone inside, not even turning once to glance back as he slid the glass door closed behind him, Glatz looked to the table, to the vial of antidote left so close to him in cruel and impossible distance.

The front door was still gaping wide and Koji and Tru were stood close enough to feel the cool air on their backs. The dust from Rahul Gupta's car had receded from view and they were left looking at Lobo's Barakudo and its one passenger seat.

"You should ask him," said Koji.

"I don't know what to do anymore. I'm thinking I'm too late for my sister. I'm considering going north back to the city."

"You never called her."

"No, I can't."

"Then you should have ridden with Mo."

"Yeah." She sat again at the side of the steps. "Maybe we should just get going back to Blua Haveno, go straight to that cop there, Wilford Lebeau. I know him, a little. Just tell everything."

"Oh no." Lobo was stood behind them in the doorway. "Never go to the police for help. There are no good cops, they are just little springs and cogs. Simply they do their function or they break, there is no good in the equation. They help you if it will look good on their record, and the opposite if it gets them the same result. Yes they would love to be on your side, so they tell you. Really it is all out of their hands. The mechanism dictates. You think a person signs up to the police to look after people? They dream to crack villainous skulls, to drive the car, to iron the uniform, to fondle the firearm. They want to be above you. Perhaps at school they felt hard done by, squashed in the lower echelons of the pyramid, or perhaps they were at the top and had already become addicted to doling out justice with impunity. Each cop, even by considering a life in that service, is in his heart born as something of a bastard. No, never go to the police with your troubles." He came down the steps past them. "And so, one of you would like to ride back to Kratera?"

"You wouldn't want to drive her down to the harbour town, would you?"

"Sorry to say, no. I am leaving now. My business takes me urgently in the other direction."

Koji looked to Tru. "Well, there's your chance."

Tru waited a beat, and if her shoulders slumped they did so bare perceptibly, and that was enough for Lobo to see. He walked to his car.

"Well, I will be going." He placed his bag in the

passenger seat and went around and got in and started his car and with a little wave of his hand he thrummed the engine out along the road and he too was gone from their company.

"Why didn't you go?"

"His little talk about cops. He's disgusting, and boring too. I don't think I could stand a drive all the way to Kratera being lectured off that bulbous prick."

Koji smiled and he'd done that so little that the face looked new to Tru.

"So, Mister Ichida, now what?"

"Ishida."

"Huh?"

"I feel stupid going back inside now. We already said goodbye."

"So we start walking again."

"That's what it looks like. Back out to the highway. Plenty more people driving this time of day, we'll get our ride. Who knows, maybe we'll even get picked up by your harbour cop."

The journalist had given up, was heading back to the crossroads on her motorcycle, an eighties Laverda Jota. There she'd wait for those two others to join her. By quitting out first she'd agreed to give up top credit on the article to the reporter. Time to let him out of the shadows if that meant she got a fresh cup of coffee out of it.

She'd recognised the woman, Tru or Alice Beatty. She wasn't sure which was presenting as which gender anymore. A pair of artists whose star had been falling year on year for a good decade now. And now what? It looked like one of those twins was hitting bottom, but what exactly that bottom was all about was beyond her fathoming, for now.

When Mitch and Lyn finally gave up on staking the David place she'd convince them to head down to the harbour town with her and visit the other sister, Alice or Tru.

She'd nearly gone south to Blua Haveno straight off. In her younger days she would have. There was a cruel mantra that did the rounds, if you wanted the real story you had to 'ditch Mitch.' She couldn't bring herself to do that to him. And in this moment she knew it was over for her, the edge was gone.

She swore into the heat, coughed and caught some phlegm in her throat, turned her head to the side, pushed up the visor on the open-faced helmet and pulled her bandana down, and when she spat something out there in the scenery caught her attention.

She pulled up the motorcycle to the side of the road and turned off the engine and got off and looked out to where she thought she had seen the figure.

On the road behind her a car came bowling along at a good pace and passed her. A blue Barakudo kicking up a good dust cloud for her to move away from and so pushing her to start walking out into the scrub as the car continued away in its dusty flight.

Timmy Bridges watched the car, the flesh around his left eye fattened, the socket fractured, the eye useless. The other struggled to focus. And then from the road he saw her emerging from the wake of dust like an angel.

She walked out a few steps towards him and stopped to take in the shambling monstrosity. His clothes once blue were blooded and layered over in dust, his hands and face too, and if she hadn't seen him stumble he'd have phased right into his backgrounds invisibly.

She stood unable to gather words to greet the vision and it was Timmy that went first with the word water.

She hurried into her satchel and then stopped. "I don't have any."

He came on, his neck stiff and one shoulder slightly raised and frozen, the arm below limp and tucked into his shirt. She backed away from the creature and still could not muster the asking words about what had happened.

As he came to her she stepped backwards and he carried on walking to the road. She followed in closely and went to put her hand on him for support but didn't know where to and withdrew her hands. She checked the highway and saw nothing either direction. "You think you can ride with me? Can you manage that?"

Timmy stopped and looked at her and she saw the half of his mouth that was hanging open and saw some teeth missing there. The heat of the day was sucking out the moisture from his mouth by the second, and even out here in the scrublands an industrious fly had made a life of things, and in lieu of much other action had been drawn to that hole like a

157

rich oasis.

He drew his good hand up and batted at the fly. It circled and landed again, bothering along that broken lip-line.

"Oh man, you must be something to do with those other three."

"Where?" His word came weak but aggressive.

"I'm sorry?"

He loomed closer to her, the voice louder and agitated. "Where?"

Taking a step back she found her words caught and then release in a wobble, "Up at the David place. Lambert David. You know who that is?"

He grunted. He turned and started towards her motorcycle and she walked a few steps behind him.

"If you think you couldn't hold on to me all the way up, we can wait and flag someone down."

"David."

"What? No? We need to get you to hospital." Her eyes fell onto the back of his jeans and to the waistline where a revolver was wedged. As if sensing her eyes he turned on her and reached with that good hand and took out that revolver that had been tucked into that canvas shroud with him, put there by Esther Moses.

The journalist turned and ran scampering away into the brush. The revolver had four empty chambers already and three of those bullets were still embedded inside his person.

He wedged the gun back this time into the front of his waistline and he went to the motorcycle and looked at the lady still running away and she ran well.

He put up the stand and started the cycle and with his one good hand he turned it back south and rode.

She watched him go. He wasn't shy in flexing the bike's muscle. By the time the dust had resettled her breath was back and she started a slow walk back to the road in a great lethargy. As a hostage at least she'd still be in the story.

In the bag that Mo had left behind they had found a flask and it even had some water left in it and they felt slighted that she had kept that from them in the night.

The flask had a strap to be hung over a shoulder and now Koji wore it so. He had the cap off already as they reached the highway and took his first slug, that walk down from the David place already breaking him into sweat.

"Here." He handed the flask out to Tru. She stood surveying the farthest reaches of the highway, as yet seeing no civilian car to be their saviour, nor cop vehicle to seal their damnation.

She shifted Mo's duffle bag on her shoulder and took the flask. After guarding the bag so closely the whole night it was curious that Mo had ridden away with her man Rahul and left it behind. Inside they'd found a box of surgical gloves, a roll of wire, wire cutters, a roll of tape, the flask, and a sawn-off

shotgun. And now Tru's handbag was inside as well.
"That's getting heavy, isn't it?" said Koji. "Not too late to ditch it. I still don't think it's a good idea."

She took off the bag and put it at her feet and Tru drank heavily of the flask and gave it back.

"You want to stay a free man, don't you?"

"My mind's coming apart. Can we go over it all again?"

"Look, this is much easier even than that dog story. What don't you get?"

"Alright, I'll go over it again. We drive along, we hit a guy standing in the road. When we get out Mo takes us both hostage to help her bury the body, because she already had it in for him. And then she marches us through the night. It doesn't make sense that we didn't tell Herbert Glatz after she left though."

"Look, I just want to get to my sister."

"No, what are we doing? We just go back and wait and wait for Glatz' driver to get back and take us home. You go to your sister. I go to the cops I suppose."

"I can't do it anymore, I can't wait, Koji. You do what you want. You don't have to be following me around like this little guard dog lost puppy. What, because you gave me the lift that ruined my life you think that I'm your ward until I get home?"

She watched him take the small towel from his

neck, rinsed out but still grubby, and dab at himself with it and knew she'd hit some kind of truth maybe he had not known himself. She took the page of newspaper from her back pocket and gave it to him.

He took it and unfolded it. "What's this?" He read the headline, looked at the picture of the pendant, held it up close to his face. "Hega Kalson? Who is that? That your pendant? Trevor told me about that. That's why he wasn't sure he said the name right when he first saw you, said also that's why you dumped him in the first place."

"I barely knew him. Another time, another life."

"Look, I can't read this you know. It's too small. You remember I was wearing glasses when we met. My eyes can't see much better than my mind right now."

"He was our agent, and I shot him yesterday afternoon. And Alice knew nothing about that and now she'll have the cops up her arsehole and she'll be in a jail cell. She's practically an agoraphobe. And now I've done this to her."

"This just gets better. Who ever wanted to be a stupid lighthouse keeper?"

"You're quite something, Koji. You never helped me out of kindness. You aren't walking me to my door out of any concern for me. It's all about you. Your sense of chivalry, how that makes you feel, or because it's just the thing you're supposed to do. All you really care about is looking after your pristine sense of yourself as a fine example of manhood."

"Yeah? That's exactly what Mo preyed on in me. She sucked it out like an animal, made me feel it was my fault for doing her murder. You too. The both of you getting exactly what you want me to do. Why did you shoot this . . . " he pulled the sheet of newspaper close to his face again and squinted at the headline, " . . . Hega Kalson?"

"Does it really matter? You'd suspect he was a bad man if someone would take the time to travel to the city just to go and shoot him, wouldn't you?"

"You might." He screwed up the paper and tossed it at her and it hit her chest and fell to the floor.

She bent and picked it up and unscrunched it, smoothed it and folded it again, then returned it to her pocket and they stood and looked at each other a while.

"No more questions? How is it me that shot him if it's my sister's half of the pendant they found at the scene?"

"What were those reasons for crime we discussed last night? Money? Psychopathy?"

"Oho. Now we see the man you are. You forgot the last one, passion. Now we see who you were all along, and exactly who we picked you out to be. Your bloom wilts under the sun, quite a thing to see." He started to talk but the sentence came out as a stifled noise, so incandescent he was, the blood in his throat visibly pumping now. He took the flask of water from his shoulder and put it on the ground before him and then he turned to head back to the house.

Tru picked up the flask. "Oh, true to form. The frail chivalry."

He gave her a last look and then carried on walking.

And while they'd been talking the journalist's motorbike had been tearing up the highway and they'd not seen it coming but now they heard it thrumming and looked to see the dust cloud spawning in its wake.

Koji carried on walking and called back, "There's your ride. Some beefcake saviour for you. Good luck." And under his breath he added, "Good riddance."

He heard the bike slowing as it approached the turn-off and he didn't look back to watch, not until he heard the bike spill, the rider trying to turn in too sharply for the speed he was travelling.

He ran back and joined Tru and there they saw a figure laying with a leg still under the bike, so coated in filth and dust that they could not instantly fathom it was the ghost of the man they'd buried that night before. He was not moving. They watched a moment, listening to the chug of the bike turning over.

"It's him," said Tru.

"It is. It is him," said Koji. "Is it him?"

"It's him."

"I can't believe it."

"It's him."

"How can it be? You remember him that well? It was dark."

"What are you talking about? Look at the state of him, Koji. Who else would it be?"

"I don't know. Coincidences do happen."

"What? No they don't."

"What do you mean they don't?"

"You just think they do. It's bound to happen. That's just numbers. Not magic."

"I never said coincidence is magic."

"There's no such thing. What about the person who was never here who we never met?"

"Tru, what are you talking about?"

"You bump into someone again and you think it's a miracle. But there's someone else who walked right past, or who had an accident, and you never got to meet them. So there was never any coincidence about it."

"You're not making any sense."

"There might have been three of us in your car last night, but there was only two."

"Not with your luggage, no room."

"That's not what I mean. I know what I mean, you're just too tired to make sense of it."

"It's not the time."

They both took a step back when they saw the man move. Timmy Bridges raised his good eye and saw. He saw these two for the first time, quite unrecognising Tru from the crossroads, now in a different outfit to boot, but he did see the duffel bag. He mumbled the name of Moses.

Tru crouched and put the flask down and harried at the zip already open on the duffel bag, making that hole bigger so she could wrestle from its place that shotgun that Mo had carried all through that long night.

"Tru! No!" Were the words Koji managed but his feet did not move him to stop her and he watched as she levelled the gun on the horrible apparition sat horizontally upon the bike.

Bridges pulled his gun also and Koji turned and ran and then stopped because Tru had not followed.
Bridges raised the pistol but his arm was behind the orders he sent into it and it wavered and Tru had her weapon pushed into her shoulder and readied before his and let rip.

The shotgun exploded in her hands, some horrendous backfire in the rigged weapon. The scream from Tru came more animal than person. The mess of her dropped.

Bridges let his gun fall onto the road and reached fruitlessly in the direction of the flask of water, one leg still pinned and immovable under the bike.

Tru quivered, a sound came from her, a bubbling drowning sound, her vocal cords butchered adding some high pitched whining to it.

Koji came to her. The backfire had torn through her shoulder, separating it from her body. The head was near detached but the eyes were still going. They saw him. He knelt into the blood pooling heavily across and off the edge of the tarmac into the hungry dust.

He took Tru's head in his hands and it moved in a way it should not. Koji raised the head up and it came away from the body and if Tru Beatty had any last sound to make it was obliterated by Koji Ishida's scream, ringing primal across the landscape.

It was not a year to the day, but it was close. Trevor Bachelet entered a wide and walled courtyard, traversed it through the sun, and walked up the steps to the Krateran Museum of Art and stopped half way up, passing into the shade of the Modernist block in front of him. He took a pack of cigarettes from his front shirt pocket and lit it with a match from a book of matches bearing the address and emblem of one of the late night joints he had played a set at in the last week, having thrown in recently with an Ethiopian jazz ensemble.

He stood facing the building and watched as the few people came out or went in, in ones and twos, and it looked like he was there waiting for someone inside to come out and meet him but he was not. By the entrance large upright banners fluttered weakly in a warm air; the one on the left emblazoned vertically with AL BEATTY, the one on the right bearing the name of the show IMPOSTEROUS.

Trevor dropped his cigarette and squashed it and looked at the other visitors and not one knew his face that had been adorning walls all across the city for the past fortnight and he went up the stairs and went in.

In the main exhibition space he wandered between the paintings, hung in a zig zag of corridors to walk between, lit starkly by lights above the pathway in an otherwise blacked out room. It put the visitors in the dock as much as the paintings, disconcertingly picking at the top of your eyebrows as you blinked into and out of the cones of light, each designed to make a sphere that included two paintings on the black walls either side.

The show had been on near three weeks, was at its quietest now, as many of the folks who took in that side of its culture escaped the city in the hottest months. The final flurry of visitors would come next week when those who were tardy but also scared of missing out would boost the twilight numbers. Now there were just a few others walking ahead of Trevor through the corridors of paintings, mostly tourists only half interested going through the motions.

He watched them occasionally stopped in the shadow between the cones of light to look at the pictures. That would have been Alice's intention. If you wanted to look directly at the works, you'd have to be on stage yourself, you'd have to stand right inside the light.

They didn't stop for long, just the customary time they felt was necessary for having paid to come in, and as they walked further he noticed they stopped for less time, their minds moving already to how they'd talk about the paintings to their friends after they were back out into the daylight.

Would they go first and risk embarrassing themselves with an opinion, or wait to hear on what their pals thought? To then agree without question, or be contentious for the sake of it, if that was what their ego required of them. Most of these people came to galleries just to—

He caught himself in the derisory thoughts, his smile-sigh a self mockery as he reached for his cigarettes in habit and stopped his hand on his pocket.

Was this why he'd pulled out of his return concert? Had he so little belief in anyone's ability to experience his art? He imagined them out there in the dark as he played, enjoying being the kinds of people who went to that kind of thing, rather than hearing his music, really hearing it.

Better to play easy-listening in a restaurant or an after-hours club, to be the background, to be occasionally drowned out by explosions of laughter, or be a soundtrack to a lone drinker's sad ruminations.

Well that was all he had left to him now. He'd let a lot of people down, a lot of players in Kratera he'd dried up his favours with. They might still book him for their private parties. Now he really was an exhibit. His grand failure might even put him in higher demand. Though on a lower pay grade, he'd still have his rent and smoking money.

Trevor stopped a moment at the end of one of the corridors, looked back and saw no-one coming up behind, and let those ahead move on. He stopped himself in one of those patches of light and knew Alice's purpose in the design. He knew that feeling, being inside that specific stark stage lighting, and he knew how carefully she'd chosen it.

He chose one of the paintings that flanked him and looked at it. A gold frame, a background as black as the walls they were hung on, and painted in golds a figure adorned each painting. Each clothed the same way, but each pose different, one here with its hands in its pockets, one there scratching its head, or with its hands clasped in front of it and so the variations went on from one frame to the other. Each subject he had seen before just the once, in that pit, in that cave underneath the Lambert David residence, on that night close to a year ago to the day.

There was purpose too in this hanging, that behind you you'd feel the other golden effigy of Glatz staring into your back, and somehow you felt that other person would be more interesting than this one you were looking at. And you'd never be able to see both at once, to flick your eyes from one to another. You'd have to turn about-face and in that movement the memory of the other was already faded.

Someone moved in his periphery coming up behind him in the circuit. He looked there but saw no persons. They must have stopped in one of those dark patches. He felt watched and moved off, casually walked his way through the rest of the show and left and found himself back out on the steps.

The sun had moved the shadow and he stood inside it again but further down than before and he reached again for his cigarettes. There were less people than before and he heard the footsteps of one of them coming down behind him and the besuited person stepped down into the sun and turned and looked at him from under a broad-brimmed hat that felt out of place in the city, and the hat belonged to the cop from Blua Haveno, and it took Trevor a good few seconds to place him, being so in this place unexpectedly.

"Lebeau?"

"Mister Bachelet."

"A little out of your jurisdiction aren't you? You came to see this?" He gestured at the museum behind them with a match and then lit his cigarette.

"This? Naw. Art's not my bag. Seems to me that people come to look at themselves more than anything else, and I can do that anywhere, all of my own accord. Was it any good?"

"It's good. She's good. She's back on her game. You should go in and have a look."

"She? Oh I did."

"And yet you didn't come to see it."

"Nope. Just happened to be passing by, and I saw you, and then I saw her name written up there big." He looked up at the banners barely fluttering. "His? Theirs? Confusing isn't it."

Trevor smoked. Lebeau turned and sat on a step and took his hat off and wafted himself with it and put it back on and stayed with his back to Trevor as he talked.

"From what I gather, it was Alice you used to go with first."

"Long time ago."

"Then you took off with her sister, Tru."

"They didn't go by those names back then."

"Confusing, isn't it. I suppose that was the game."
"Artists."

"I heard that Tru was the twin actually born male?"

Trevor shuffled his feet, looked around the courtyard, waited. Lebeau went on:

"They both presented as female when you were

mixed up with them. They even went under the knife and you'd be hard pressed to tell one from the other. I suppose you know they even had their fingerprints altered to match?"

"How would that work?"

"Oh? You know anything's possible in Kratera if you have the coin for it."

"I know what you're doing, Lebeau."

"She hadn't gone all the way yet, back then. Tru that is. Not until she took off, took off with you. And it was when she was with you that she did go all the way and got the final operation."

"It must be hard for someone basic and crude like yourself to come to get to grips with it. Funny how fascinated you are by it. It's all you people obsessed with the details, it's you with the hangups."

Lebeau turned and met his eyes and then turned away again. "I've got no problem with it. The detail that I found curious is how you two broke off the engagement, the night of the engagement party."

"If you heard so much, sounds like you know more than I do. Should be me asking the questions."

"That's funny, because I haven't actually gotten to the questions yet. I'm just talking. Just talking about how Alice was there at the engagement party as well. Hell of a pair of . . . whatever you want to call them. How must that have felt?"

"That's the question?"

"For Alice I mean. How must have that have felt to see your man run away with your brother? Must be understandable. I mean, he has something you don't, right? But then, he gets that changed as well."

Lebeau made a whistle. "Wow. That must have stung. Not only was your twin more a man than you could ever be, now she's more a woman as well."

Trevor dropped his cigarette beside Lebeau, left him in the smoke floating up from it as he walked down the steps past him.

"Here's my question, Mister Bachelet." Trevor walked on and Lebeau raised his voice across the space to turn a head or two amongst the very few who were traversing the courtyard. "How come you didn't recognise her?"

Trevor stopped and came back and stood below the harbour cop. "You didn't happen to see me, did you? I think you came here especially. You got cut out of a loop after Lambert David went away. Now you're just a straight cop because no one needs you bent. And all you've got is a lot of time to think about your fuck ups. What are you trying to do? Who you trying to impress now?"

"Seems odd, that's all, to be engaged to a person, and then you can't tell that who it is you're talking to is the person's sister." Lebeau watched Trevor's face, saw him going inside his memories, then stood up and adjusted the waistline of his trousers. "No, I see it. You didn't have a clue. Looks like I was wrong about you." This time it was Lebeau who walked away, brushing Trevor as he passed him.

Trevor held onto Lebeau's arm. "You came here to see if I was in on it? That murder of their agent? How would that work out?"

"No, I didn't think you were in on it." He removed his arm from Trevor's grip and brushed imaginary dust from it. "I did think you might be covering. Now I think you are just too damn stupid to have put it together."

"You've got that all worked out from what?"

"Just from you."

"Just from me."

"That's right, just from you. Such a shame, that those vault robbers hit that dog that night. One imperfect crime quite unrelated and getting in the way of what would have been such a perfect crime."

Wilford Lebeau walked away down the steps and Trevor Bachelet sat down upon the steps and took out his cigarettes.

Two weeks later Trevor Bachelet was in Blua Haveno, same time that his comeback concert would have been on, his jazz ensemble sympathetic to his hiatus. He'd taken a room above a bric-a-brac shop overlooking the harbour. In the early evenings he sat at his window with the shutters open and smoked and watched the bustle as city escapers perused the bars and cafes, returned from the islands on the last ferries. In the later evening he'd take a walk and hope for a cool air off the sea and after eating would then take a drink or so in the bars.

In the mornings he'd take his coffee down there in the streets and he'd not seen her either in the days or the nights. A couple of times he'd walked up through the town to the hill that overlooked it and walked on hard dirt roads between the large wooden houses of the permanent residents.

Her house was painted white with blue trim. He

stopped by the gate once or twice, the gate of the house that belonged to that cousin of theirs who had put up the twins here for the last decade, been their refuge. He looked up to the large attic where she used to keep her studio space with her sister, and perhaps worked there now as he looked. The circular window was repurposed from part of an old bomber, the many panes making for many reflections and impossible to see inside of.

If she had seen him he hadn't felt her eyes and she hadn't come out to him so he'd passed by. Perhaps tomorrow he'd go to the door. Or the day after.

Wilford Lebeau kept his office at the far end of the harbour. His feet were up on his desk and he read the newspaper and didn't look up when Trevor came in the door and stopped before the low wooden fence that separated Lebeau's area from that permitted for the public. Trevor stood with his hands in his pockets for a moment.

When he took them out Lebeau said, "Don't start your smoking in here."

"Shouldn't you be pretending to do some work?"

Lebeau looked over the newspaper. "This is my work. Knowing the news is a cop's work, isn't it?" He swung his feet down and crumpled the news-paper down onto his desk. "You been to see her yet?"

"No, not yet. I don't think I will."

"Come in, Bachelet." He offered his hand to the chair opposite his desk.

"Trevor," he said as came through the low gate.

"Wilford then," said Lebeau. "And don't get ideas that I believe what I read in these lines of text they print in the papers. The job is the reading in between them."

Lebeau took a jug with ice and cucumber and lemon slices in it and poured a glass but just for himself.

Trevor sat and said, "I'm surprised you didn't know I was in town."

"Oh I did."

"No hello?"

"I know you've been up to the house a couple of times. I know you haven't been in yet."

"She tell you that?"

"Why don't you go and ask her?"

"I don't know who I'd be asking."

"Now you're getting it."

"I can't say it's my problem."

"And yet here you are, just on holidays?"

"Something like that."

"If I was to ask which of us in the room was more humiliated by all that's been going on, which name would you proffer up?"

"I don't think I'd know the answer to that."

"I might say it was the one who's been renting a room above the main drag there."

"I might say it was someone who came all the way up to Kratera just to rouse a man up because he's out of ideas."

"It's true a man from here might have other business in the city from time to time, why not kill a second bird while he's at it?"

"It's true a city man needs some sea air once in a while as well." Trevor looked around. There was a second smaller desk and that had Lebeau's hat on it. "You have to get some help in when you're out of town?"

"They do let me have time off you know. Yes I have a lazy deputy. Even has a uniform."

"So what kind of work do you have for a humiliated man?"

Lebeau poured a second glass and pushed it across the table.

It was mid-morning and he stood by the harbour wall from the bric-a- brac shop. He had his holdall packed and that was on the wall beside him and he smoked and watched the people walking to and fro and soon he'd head off to the bus stop and be on his way back up to the city and then he saw her.

She sauntered casually to the window of the shop and peered through the myriad squares of glass at the beachcomber junk that was the fare of the shop. She wore a shirt that helped disguise her gender, and slacks, and her dark hair was cut short, and she wore no make-up. Immaculate and perfectly androgynous.

Trevor's gut was tight and the smoke wasn't a help then and he tossed it over the wall and she turned her head and looked directly at him, so he thought, but then she turned and carried on away in that same casual lope that had brought her here.

Perhaps she had just felt his eyes. It was a sensitivity

that had developed in himself after he'd become a known face. Not so much in these later years, but the sense of being seen had never really gone away. You'd look around suddenly and directly at someone, convinced they were onto you, but was it not just the movement of your head that brought them to you? The flick of a cigarette over a sea wall?

Even down here in Blua Haveno he'd seen the looks a couple of times in those bars at night. But the folks who would recognise him didn't belong to a world where approach was on their agenda. Once or twice someone would lean over to their partner and a second head would turn. But were they just wondering about who was this cat who kept eyeballing them? He wondered if two semi-famous has-beens had ever fallen into a feedback loop of glances, neither knowing the other, both thinking they were the one getting the stare down.

There was no way she hadn't recognised him. No way. He took up his bag and did not walk the direction of the bus but instead did follow her through the streets at a distance. She stopped for coffee and sat outside and he went behind her and inside the cafe and sat by the window and watched her, lost in her thoughts so it seemed, and not looking around for him.

A young couple approached her and he watched

her smile and engage in smalltalk and the girl produced a small book from a bag and offered a pen over and Alice obliged and drew something inside it. The couple spoke to her a little more when it was done. Mostly it was them talking. Nerves. And then they went off and he saw them happy and the girl opened the book and studied what had been put there. Now she had a little piece of Alice and she gripped the book in both hands and held it to her chest.

Alice sat impassive again, not watching them as they walked away, a veteran of being accosted for plunder, to giving away another little piece of herself, and she was back in her own thoughts.

When she left Trevor left as well and walked behind her twenty yards and dropped back further when she started up the hill to her home on those baked dirt roads, walking on the shaded side of the street. Turning a corner he saw her enter her gate and then went back to a spot he'd seen where he could empty his bladder and then he went back and he walked to the gate and looked at the house she had gone into and he put down his bag that had started an ache into his shoulder and he put his hand on the gate but he didn't open it. He rubbed at his shoulder and stooped to collect his holdall and when he stood he saw her rested against a tree in the front yard.
"You want some lemonade?"

"I would." Trevor opened the gate and went in and walked to her. "How are you, Alice? Alice alright to call you by? You're going by Al again, right?"

"Alice is alright. I thought I might see you at the opening."

"No invite."

"Oh." She walked towards the house. "Go around the back, I'll come out to you."

He sat in the garden at the back of the house on a painted metal chair beside a painted round metal table, surrounded by broad leafed plants and in the shade of a tree evolved to warm climes. She came with a tray that had a jug on it and glasses.

"I did go and see the show though. I prefer to go when it's quieter anyway."

"The opening was trash. Horrible. I avoid Kratera as much as possible now."

"Just like Tru."

"She didn't even leave this town for five years. You know that?"

"Not until she did."

"No, and look where that got her."

"You know that Wilford Lebeau is on your case?"

"That why you finally came to see me?" She opened an extra button of her shirt and played at an itch on her collarbone. He took the cue to look at the pendant she wore, both masks interlocked and reunited as a single necklace.

"Must have been hard to get that back."

"Not so hard, once it all blew over."

"He thinks you aren't Alice. He thinks you're Tru. He thinks you two were conspiring to make it impossible for a court to nail either one of you, in case they were sending down the wrong twin. You weren't ever worried about getting nailed on a conspiracy?"

Alice smiled. "He's quite the bored little cop."

"Red faced little cop. Being stuck down here on the take was alright for him. Now he's just stuck down here. Maybe he thinks you're his way out."

"What's wrong with here?"

"Fine if you're a painter. Tru was always the better painter, but that was quite a show you put on. Those golden Glatz.' How did you get in to see the statues before they got buried?"

"I didn't. It was from photos."

"Glatz made it to the opening?"

"He was."

"How was he?"

Alice thought on it. "At least half there."

"So is it true that Hega Kalson was going to go public and humiliate you for being a front, while poor Tru was the recluse and working up there signing your name on her work? That why you did him in?"

"Sure. Why not? I found out he's been blackmailing her for favours. Could have just as well been me that did him in. Just a race to the punchline. You believe that?"

They drank and were quiet a moment.

"Why did Lebeau send you in here?"

"You mean why did he want to send me in here?"

"That's what I meant."

"All I'd have to do is get close to you again and then ask some questions about private things that I knew only one or the other of you would know the answer to, and that would be that."

"We never had many secrets from each other."

"She know you headed down to the city to bump off Kalson?"

"She did that all by herself, dressed up as herself. Can you believe that?"

"Something doesn't add up, but I never was any good at counting. I suppose I was always too lazy to do the work."

"How did it feel seeing Glatz up there in gold? They said you were one of the last to ever see him before the incident. Before is maybe not the word. You were right there. His tormentor was sat right there in front of you and you didn't even see it."

"Glatz really did tell you everything, didn't he. Who approached who about doing your show?"

"I forget, it just came about."

Trevor tugged at his shirt pocket to take out his cigarettes and stopped. "I never felt bad about Glatz. Nor about your sister. I mean yes, of course, I felt bad about it. I never felt that I had any hand in being able to stop it. If I'd done this, or if I'd done that. Things I could never have guessed at, because I didn't. What kind of fool lives like that?"

"Pretty much most of everyone."

"That how you feel about your sister doing in Kalson?" He took out his cigarettes. "I wonder if they ever found that assassin? I'd ask Lebeau but he just got fed what was in the papers like everyone else is, is what I'd bet. A rare toxin in seafood, some puffer fish or whatever it was they pinned it on." He popped a cigarette from the pack of Krakens and pointed it up towards the top of the house. "What are you working on?"

"Come up and see?"

"I'd love to." He put the cigarette behind his ear and followed her up to the house.

She sat on a wicker two-seater and let him wander between the works and watched him, never long between one and the next.

"You used a mirror for each one?"

"Yes."

"So it's not really her, it's you." After he had said that he seemed to spend longer observing the works, somehow letting it divorce himself from the subject. "Still, I don't know how you could."

Each work was a head decapitated. This one a circular painting in a classical style, the decapitated head that of Medusa but with the twins' face. Another next to it done in a hellish vision that would have befit Bacon, the eyes and mouth dark blurred maws. This one here done in intricate pencils, the face bereft of emotion, the neck sliced cleanly, the background etched into blackness. The next was a horrible photomontage of tarmac and her head but as with all the others the hairstyle was Tru's. Offal from roadkill spilled from the neck. There was no body. Stopping at an anime-styled rendering of the violent moment, with speed lines and sounded with onomatopoeia in lettering he couldn't read, he'd had his fill.

He joined her and slumped down next to her on the seat. "And this is helpful to you? Is this getting your demons out?"

"Who said I had demons? I'll have a hell of an audience. Maybe that's what I'll call it. Hell Of An Audience."

Trevor played with his palms as if studying the lines there would prevent him from having to look around the room again. "I don't think I'll make it to the opening of that one."

"Are you shocked by my attitude? You think I

should play the demons angle when they quiz me? A thousand artists would, a million. And each would be talking to cover up what they had, what every artist wants, to be looked at. The more they talk the more they fool themselves. Maybe I shouldn't talk at all."

"It would add to the theatre if you didn't, but the critics will get frustrated at you. They'll turn on you, start making things up, maybe try to wreck you all over again."

"True enough. Maybe I'll call it that. True Enough. How should I spell it?"

"You want to know what I think?"

"Honestly? Not really."

"Then you are the real deal. Or you're damn clever at pretending to be." He couldn't help himself, his eyes drawn back to the works. "You always were honest to the T, that I couldn't doubt of you. Maybe honest isn't the word. Straightforward. Except when you two dressed up as each other, swapped out your pendants." He took the cigarette that still sat behind his ear and put it in his mouth.

She took it out of his mouth and put it in her own shirt pocket. "I'll be honest enough to say we had a cruel streak as well. So you want to ask me and get it over with?"

"Ask you what?"

"Was it me that did in Kalson?"

"I thought you already told me that."

"Was it Tru pretending to be me like the cops believed, just to tie things up and get the case closed? The abused sister, a prisoner caught between her twin and her agent. They had a killer to pin it on and now the killer was dead, story over, everyone goes home. Or had Tru found out what I had planned to do but she didn't get there in time, and it was too late. And I made it back to Kratera, but she didn't, because she can't drive and she missed her bus?"

"I should get going, I'll miss the next bus north, and I already checked out of my room. It's been took already for tonight. Busy moment there in town, this time of season."

"Stay a night more if you want to, here."

"Your cousin away?"

"Always."

"Alright, can I take your cousin's room instead of Tru's?"

"That's one rule we don't break. I tell you what, you take my room and I'll take Tru's."

"You alright with that?"

"I'm alright with this," she threw her hand around the room, "So I suppose so."

"Is her room how she left it?"

"Yeah, pretty much. You want to see?"

"No."

The sheets of Alice's bed had a mustiness about them. Though clean, they hadn't been slept in for some time. He never mentioned it the next day or in the days or fortnight following. He continued on in his stay, not yet needed back in the city, and while she worked on the gruesome portraits he took walks down to the town. He made dinners for her and made sure she came down to eat them. Some days she would eat with a distant look on her, and he knew that look, he'd known it being on his own face when he had been a composer. His comeback show was to be a little Bach with mostly his own material to top the bill, but it was old works. The look she bore he might never again.

There was no piano in this house and he wasn't bothered either way about that, though a couple of times he had taken to the keys in one of the bars down in the town, raucous and upbeat for the midnight crowd.

On his last night Alice had come down the hill with him and they'd drank and it had felt like when they'd first met, or at least with the intervening years chopped out and these two eras sewn back together. That was the only time he'd seen Lebeau make his presence known, for some brief time propping an end of the bar, but they hadn't gotten into any converse.

They had walked arm in arm back up the hill and had organically returned to their own beds. Trevor wondered if that might not be an accurate depiction of some couple who had been together as long as they would have, had he not been so savagely shown the door in their past.

The next day he sat in the back garden at the metal table and drank orange juice and read the Daily Krateran.

"Good morning." She came and sat, hair still damp, towel on her shoulder.

"Thought you'd never be up. How's your head?"

"Not ideal. I'm not the veteran at those late nights like you."

"Oh, I don't know, that's some late hours licks you put in when you're in flow up in that attic there."

"Minus the booze."

"Can I come up and see yet?"

"Not yet."

"How come you let me in before?"

"Because I thought you were leaving."

"You did?"

"Maybe not." She took his orange juice and drank it. "I don't feel like working today. You feel up for driving?"

"I could do. I'm rusty. I don't think I've driven since we were together."

"That long? That's crazy. I'm sure it comes back. If you were away from the keys ten years, how would that work out?"

He took some time to think on that. "I'd be rusty. It's safer if you drive I'd say."

"I wouldn't say that."

"Head that bad is it?"

"No, I don't drive."

"No? I could barely get you out from behind the wheel when we were a unit. I was already rusty even before we split."

"You're thinking about Tru." She watched him think on it and interrupted his memories, "I lost my nerve."

"You did? When?"

"Hard to say. It started after Tru went. I look pretty together. I'm not."

He folded the paper and plopped it on the table and stood. "Let's get some breakfast."

"I'm not ready to eat yet. Let's do up a basket

He drove her rusted Skarabo out of Blua Haveno and a little way up the coast and they came to the lighthouse and in its side shaded from the sun they sat in the grasses above the rocks and watched the sea and ate their picnic on a blanket.

As they finished the sun was coming around the side of the lighthouse. Trevor had been looking up at the tower and when he looked back Alice had shuffled in closer to him to give her a few more minutes out of the heat.

He asked her, "Did you keep in touch with that guy?"

"Who are you on about?"

He thumbed at the lighthouse. "You know. That guy."

"You forgot his name?"

"I did."

"So did I. You'd think I'd have his name etched into

memory. The man whose hands put Tru out of the world."

"I wouldn't say he'd had much choice in it."

"Oh he did. A powerful guy. You wouldn't think that from seeing him."

"You saw him after the funeral?"

"No. I never knew what happened to him."

"Guy like that, goes back to his life. He just carries on."

"Don't we all?"

"I suppose we don't have much choice in that. Some of us carry on better than others."

She stood and walked closer to the edge. She took off her pendant, held it out at arms length. "I always get the urge to throw this into the sea."

"That's an important family tie, isn't it? It's just you now."

She put her arm down. "There's our cousin still, but not really our blood cousin. Anyway, that story about it being the only thing our old man ever gave us was made up." She came back from the edge and sat again. "Maybe it's time I had a kid before it gets too late in the day."

Trevor folded up the handkerchiefs that had held their sandwiches.

"I'm thinking of starting over, Trevor."

"Where would you go?"

"I mean the show."

"Wow."

"I figured if there's anyone an expert on the joy of walking away from things, it's you. So you want to talk me out of it? That's a lot of work I already put in."

"That's your decision. Not mine. You want me to talk you out of it? I think you asking me is like flipping a coin. You don't know what result you want until the coin lands. I suppose asking me is like having the coin come down on its edge."

She laughed loudly and threw her head back, stopping him from his tidying of the picnic. It was a laugh and a mannerism he hadn't heard or seen in some time.

"You get more like Tru. You noticed that?"

"I have. It's like I'm making up for her not being around by taking her into me." She held up the pendant to demonstrate the two masks united there and then put it back around her neck.

"Well I'd say at least make the works you've already done documented into a book or something. Even when I didn't perform material, I've still kept all my manuscripts."

"Yeah but you've never recorded them onto tape."
"Tape?" He smiled. "There you've a point. But don't burn those portraits. Could be in ten years you'll feel far enough away from it, you can show it under other

circumstances."

"Why give myself the dilemma? The time spent thinking it over could end up robbing me of coming on something better."

"So if you ditch it, what's next?"

"I'm changing how I want to do it. I'm going to cast my own head. I'll make a thousand rubber heads. I'll make each the weight of a real decapitated head. The audience will be allowed to lift them, throw them around, abuse them, do what they want."

"They'll get stolen."

"No bags inside policy."

"You'll get visited by two dwarfs dressed up in a long coat."

"Maybe I'll let a thousand visitors in a day. Each gets a head to take home. Every morning a chute in the ceiling will release a thousand more heads, inside a giant perspex box. One person goes in at a time, watched by the audience on the outside. A two way mirror, so all the person sees is an infinity of chopped off heads."

"Unless they are visitor number one thousand."

"Then they'll have a different experience. It will still be one."

Trevor thumbed again at the lighthouse. "Maybe you can get that fellow who was here last year to come to the opening, maybe he can start the show by firing a head out of a cannon at the exact time and date he took off Tru's real head. Or maybe you can set up an event where it's you in prosthetics and he gets to recreate the horror all over again."

"You don't like it."

"And I see you've flipped the coin and the more resistance you get from me the more you'll pursue it." The sun had reached her face, lit one of those green eyes brilliant. She came and laid down out of it and put her head in his lap and he stroked her hair.

"How's your head feeling now? Better?"

"Can you guess how heavy it is?"

He put his hands either side of her head. "Relax more. No, not really, it's kind of impossible."

"The idea is good."

"Yeah I know. It's what all you artists want, the perfect show about mortality." He put his hand down onto her collar bone and moved his fingers on that perfect skin to the pendant and held it and looked at it. "Imagine if you had twins, you could pass this on in the same way."

"I think it changed us. These two expressions we saw staring back in the mirror at us each day. Hers conceited. Mine mournful. It formed us, changed everything."

"In a way this pendant is what changed my course as well."

"You blame us for everything that happened to you after we left you?"

"You could have done it a kinder way. Was it all planned out?"

"We planned out everything."

"Everything?"

"There was never room for anyone else. We tried it out and every time it didn't work. All we wanted was each other. It was me that caught you, it was me that gave you to Tru. And you thought that was your choice. We let you think it."

"And who was it decided to throw me away?" He looked to a tan Kaprico pulling up by where they'd parked their own car back by the lighthouse. "It's Lebeau. I'd better go and talk to him."

Lebeau had his head in the door of the lighthouse when Trevor got to him. He was carrying a metal detector.

"Trev. Door's unlocked, but he's not in. You seen Ortiz?"

"You came up here looking for him?"

"What do you think?"

They looked to Alice. She sat faced away from them and out of earshot, hugging her knees and looking out to sea, her body divided down the middle by the shade of the lighthouse.

Lebeau took his hat off and fanned himself with it.

"You ready? I can take her in right now. Looks like she's had a good final moment of thinking she's got away with it."

"I couldn't imagine a nicer spot."

"So what have we got?"

"Not enough. What is it in the end? My word over hers? A scorned has been?"

"Jesus man, you didn't get the silver bullet? A ten year old could have done a better job."

"Besides all that, I've found out exactly what you didn't want to hear."

"You dick. You're going to tell me that's Al Beatty."

"They planned it out together, I couldn't fault that part. But Alice had nothing to do with going through with it. For her it was just a fantasy. She pulled out of the scheme and Tru went ahead and did Kalson without her. It might be the only time they ever truly acted independently, and look where that got them."

Lebeau put his hat back on. "Is that the way you want to play it?"

"That's the way it is. Looks like you're stuck down here a bit longer, Wil."

"You dick. You want any favours doing you, forget about putting your shape in my door." He took a couple of steps in Alice's direction, stood there a moment and then lofted his metal detector on his shoulder and went back to his car.

Trevor rejoined Alice as Lebeau pulled away and stood behind her.

She spoke with her back still turned, "There's things you've not asked me."

"There's things I won't."

"Is he going to be trouble?"

"No, I don't think so. Look, I better get back for that bus."

"Why don't you stay?"

"Obligations."

"I didn't think you were big on those."

"Depends who they're to."

"You'll come back."

THE BEMOAN

First published in 2021
This edition first published 2022
Copyright Jonathan Chandler 2021
Cover by Tyler Landry

BY THE SAME AUTHOR

Turtle Half & Cumber
Bad Man Standing
Wet Shape In The Dark
Modification
John's Worth

Printed in Great Britain
by Amazon